THE
UNFORGOTTEN

A Novella and
Other Stories

THE UNFORGOTTEN

A Novella and
Other Stories

Julia Ballerini

Columbus, Ohio

The Unforgotten: A Novella and Other Stories

Published by Gatekeeper Press
2167 Stringtown Rd, Suite 109
Columbus, OH 43123-2989
www.GatekeeperPress.com

Photo.co. Holger Trülzsch

The editorial work for this book is entirely the product of the author. Gatekeeper Press did not participate in and is not responsible for any aspect of this element.

ISBN (hardcover): 9781662909849
ISBN (paperback): 9781662909856
eISBN: 9781662909863

CONTENTS

THE UNFORGOTTEN

≈ HOW NICE TO SEE YOU

It's a time of violence, of upheavals, dispersals. Fires, floods, earthquakes, erupting volcanoes destroy dwellings and lives. People flee from countries they once called home. Throughout the world people die from a shiny new Virus. The death count is over half a million and still counting. Mercedes lives in the middle of New York City, a major epicenter of the disease: hospital tents in the park, helicopters flying above, ambulances wailing below. A Black man is killed by police for having a counterfeit bill. Protests. More killings. People pack up and leave. Many will never to return to the city they've celebrated for most of their lives.

Mercedes doesn't seem to have the Virus but it's infected her mind. The Virus colors her thoughts Orange. Code Orange.

And rage at ongoing injustice colors her thoughts Red. Blood Red.

Of Tomorrow the Mind Does Not As-Yet Know (Martha Ronk). Not As-Yet. Not so far. The poem, pre-pandemic, assumes a Tomorrow to be known, at least that's how Mercedes wants to read it. Not As-Yet.

Following her 80th birthday, celebrated shortly before the Virus came to town, a massive flareup of acute pain coursed throughout her body. A microcosmic anticipation of the worldwide flareups to come? Getting out of bed: an effort. Getting dressed: an effort. Getting up from a chair: an effort. Pliers to turn on the stove. Diagnosis: rheumatoid arthritis. Stress may be the cause, the doctor told her. Calm down, the doctor said. Steroids and medication relieved the pain, brought back her strength, but damaged her liver and kidneys. Now her white cell count is low. She's a high-risk statistic.

Alone in self-imposed quarantine, she writes. She writes letters to judges and officials respectfully asking that immigrants be released from jail and not be deported from the USA where they have made a new home. She writes stories about all kinds of places and people and things, and about her own life. Ever since she was able to put words on paper writing has been her way to survive.

≈

She remembers an early attempt to write as clearly as if she's right there visiting her grandparents' farmhouse in Rhode Island. She's in the small sitting room next to the kitchen, the room where the family gathers. From the bay window she can see fields leading down to the river in the distance. It's winter because potted geraniums bloom red on the sill, plants that flank outdoor steps in warm weather. There's a fire in the stone fireplace although she's not sure about that.

She's curled in the squishy brown ottoman chair. She hovers a pencil over a pad of blank paper on her lap. Bravo, her uncle's sleek, brown Dachshund who lost a bite-size chunk of one ear in a dogfight, is lying in front of the fireplace. (Yes, there is a fire.) Usually Mercedes coaxes him onto her lap, but at this moment she's focused on marking a sheet of paper with dashes and swirls.

Have I written a word? Have I written a word yet? She rushes into the kitchen waving her sheet of paper between her mother's face and the half-peeled potatoes in the sink. She demands to know if her scribbles are words. No dear, says her mother, barely glancing at her daughter's efforts.

Some women get erased a little at a time. Some reappear ... (Rebecca Solnit)

Decades later it was the mother who was erased a little at a time. She did not reappear. To say that she didn't recognize her daughter is no longer a metaphor.

She would sit on the edge of her bed, stare out the window at the parking lot of The Institution. How......Nice...... To......See......You, she'd slowly annunciate when she became aware that Mercedes had entered the room—her rote response to all who approached. It was not long before the mother was no longer capable of saying How......Nice......To......See...... You or any other words. Mercedes wonders if the mother ever asked herself somewhere in the far recesses of her brain, Have I said a Word? Have I said a Word yet?

By the end, when Mercedes would enter the Common Room, she'd lower her eyes, unable to face yet again the cluster of seated bodies, heads lolling in semi-baldness, faces erased of all awareness, only to be confronted by rows of ankles flopped beneath flowered quilted robes, feet slid out of tattered slippers, flaking skin wrinkled over congestions of purple veins like heavily trafficked roads seen from a descending airplane. When she raised her eyes it was she who could hardly recognize her mother.

≈

Mercedes was not erased. She reappeared over the years, slowly came into being in words on a page.

The words were always there within those first scribbles, merely unborn. It wasn't long after that moment in her grandparents' back room that they came into life wobbling and tilting on the pages like a newborn colt, spellings approximated, some letters printed backwards.

Lines and lines of words gradually becoming more upright and steady, pages and pages of words all lost, discarded, forgotten.

Still, there is one story Mercedes never, never forgets. A little girl was chopped into teensy, teensy pieces. The tiny bits of her were sprinkled all around the whole wide world. And that is why, the story concludes, hope is everywhere.

She was four or five when she wrote that story, a sickly child prone to accidents. And her father was known for his terrifying, uncontrollable rages. Yet, while dismemberment is a brutal act, she doesn't remember her story being about violence or pain. Hope. It was about hope. She was writing herself into hope. Hope far and wide. Ubiquitous hope.

She was a navy brat, an only child shuttled from place to place, country to country, language to language. She was looked after by a rotating series of indigenous servants hired by her mother who never could learn a foreign language. The maids would cuddle her and feed her forbidden sweets. She would grow attached only to be wrenched away yet again. Wrenched away? Dismemberment. Her story gets complicated.

≈

Now the onerous process of putting her home and affairs in order, begun before the Virus, has taken on new urgency. She's overwhelmed. One thing at a time, she tells herself. File cabinets. Three of them. Desk drawers. Closets, seven closets. All packed with who knows what. Bureau drawers. Bookshelves, floor to ceiling in every room. Kitchen cabinets. Why should it be so difficult to get rid of possessions? She's certainly had practice. A peripatetic childhood and a twenty-year marriage dictating multiple relocations. Divorce. Relationships. Packing, moving; discarding, letting go.

But for the past twenty years she's been settled in a commodious pre-war apartment in Manhattan. She's been able to do pretty much anything she wants: take subways to the gym, to meet friends, to outings all over town. Now, isolated by the Virus, she erases future events and appointments from her calendar one by one.

Another erasure is also occurring. Things she used to do without thinking, such as prepare breakfast, now require attention: set timer for coffee, plunge coffee press when timer goes off, put bread in toaster oven. One time she left the oven on until lunchtime. Scared the bejeezus out of her. She worries she's becoming the Mother. How......Nice......To...... See...... You. Not that she sees anyone in quarantine. Except on FaceTime and Zoom. Yoga class on Zoom is not the same.

She's about to renounce her life-long work as a translator. She's bilingual, but words in both Spanish and English have become recalcitrant, slow to surface. Her dependence on dictionaries and thesauruses has increased. She can't keep up the pace, meet deadlines.

But she can take all the time she needs to fumble for words to write stories. She writes of hard times that she has lived through, survived, even come out ahead. Resilient, she reminds herself. She's resilient.

As in the beginning when words were struggling to be born, she now struggles to keep words alive, to keep herself alive, to keep hope alive. She writes to tell herself she can beat the odds on this one too. Neurogenesis! Words will give birth to new connective neurons wobbling in the hippocampus, dentate gyrus, or wherever. She sends out her stories, her letters, her petitions—not only for immigrants but also for prisoners and postal workers, bees and bears, elephants and elms, and many more of the multitude living beings of which she is a part. She scatters teeny bits of hope here and there on a world wide web as in the tale she wrote so very long ago.

≈ THE ZONE

The idea of writing about the past prompts Mercedes to settle in her frayed reading chair with an old leather-bound atlas. She'd purchased it with her twelfth birthday money, against her mother's objections. "Dear, buy something *nice*," is what she'd said. She opens the atlas to Central America. Countries are defined in yellow, green, orange, pink, and purple. Panama is purple except for a minuscule orange segment: CANAL ZONE. The printed name splays out into the blue of the ocean, too large for the space it identifies, a*s when emotion too far exceeds its cause* (Elizabeth Bishop). Mercedes's index finger marks that tiny orange spot: her birthplace.

Panama, August 28, 1939. 6:02 p.m. Panama was teeming with documented US military and undocumented West Indians. Her father, César, a Mexican-born American citizen, was one of the additional personnel the War Department assigned to defend its vulnerable canal. That's how she came to be born in a military hospital in The Zone, a separate entity within the Canal Zone that the USA had commandeered. It was a mere slither of land, a strip of real estate ten miles wide, not counting the waterway that divided it precisely in half. Nonetheless, this instance of imperialism made her an official US citizen, even if the territory was not in the US itself. To add to the confusion of where exactly she was born, Panama itself was still embroiled in secessionist revolts from Colombia in 1939 and so wasn't exactly an established nation.

It was (and still is) an in-between place, a heterotopic place, a narrow isthmus connecting Costa Rica and Colombia, a humped strip of land jagging between the Atlantic and the Pacific. Furthermore, its claim to fame is a massive manmade rupture—a thoroughfare that the French engineer Lesseps envisioned as an act of perforation that would "prove to the world that we are males."

She was named Mercedes Prudence O'Brian, an awkward assemblage of mismatches signifying her Mexican-Irish father and her New Englander mother, Gertrude.

So then, given an incompatible name, born in a Zone that was not exactly Panama, toted on to Peru, then Cuba (a skinny island that might once have been an isthmus), shipped off to grandparents in the USA, on to Spain (this aged twenty-one of her own volition) only to come limping back to New York years later when jilted by her Barcelona lover . . .

Enrico. That first night with Enrico. No, not the night, the morning is the memory that lingers. Waking alongside him, sun struggling through tattered curtains as he lay sleeping, she didn't dare touch him, didn't dare disturb the fragile moment of bliss, the overwhelming longing she mistook for love.

So then, incongruously named, moved from The Zone to Rhode Island to Barcelona, with stops in between, is it any wonder that her personal identity has always been a bit shaky and now that she finds herself a confused and forgetful elder, her sense of who she is and who she may become is disrupted to the core. And is it any wonder that her finger searched for a tiny orange spot in an old atlas impelled by a desire to return to Panama where it all began. Return to the site that is no longer The Zone, to the Gaillard Cut now renamed Culebra after the mountain ridge it severs. Return to origins erased and renamed. Return to Peru and Cuba and wander streets haunted by ghosts of obliterated monuments?

Yes, self-quarantined in the middle of a pandemic makes actual travel impossible for a long time, perhaps forever given her state of health and the potent new Virus. But she still has words to write herself to way back then.

She will return to places of displacements and erasures, sites analogous to the displacements and erasures happening in her brain. Establish a sense of who she has become and will be against the background of what once was and is no longer. Fanciful symbolism, ersatz determinism. Yet the idea of Panama, a place of which Mercedes has no memory, nags, intrudes when she least expects it, especially now that she fears she may be already be forgetting who she is or ever was.

She's finding long-forgotten items in the process of decluttering her home so what better time to revisit the places of her past, places of her incongruous self. As old memories are unearthed along with forgotten belongings, the time has come to remember all she can remember, to piece together her incongruity, to write her own story, whatever that story may be. For Anatole Broyard terminal cancer was intoxicating; it gave him an unexpected freedom. *All your life you think you have to hold back your craziness*, he wrote, *but when you're sick you can let it out in all its garish colors.*

She's filled with an unexpected tingling joy, her mind alert, her body young again.

≈ LUISA THE UNPHOTOGRAPHED

Cross legged on the floor, Mercedes faces the battered, olive-green, military trunk she has avoided opening for the ten years since it first arrived. She slides out a flat envelope: PERU PICTURES. Please, oh God, please God let there be photographs of the maids, she murmurs. (She talks a lot to herself lately.) She knows it's unlikely even though they were the ones who cared for her, loved her, protected her, and rescued her, throughout her first ten years of life. They parented her. Yes, parented. Back then she wanted to be one hundred percent of them, fully of them. But she knew she was not, never could be. *Preciosa mariposa*, Mercedes whispers. Precious butterfly. That was what Luisa and all subsequent servants called her back then along with other endearments.

It was a maid who had found baby Mercedes when she was lost. Gertrude had left her lying on a large bed while she went off to another part of the house. When she returned to the bedroom, her baby was nowhere in sight. Her shriek brought the maids running.

"Kidnapped! Kidnapped!" she cried. Prone to panic as she was, her fears in this instance were not totally unfounded.

Foreign, white babies were occasionally abducted, although it was unlikely in The Zone where they lived, its parameters patrolled by US military.

"My baby's gone. Help, my baby's gone. Kidnapped!" Arms fluttering helplessly, Gertrude cried out the few words of Spanish she knew, "*Bebé! Ayuda*! Help! *Ayuda! Bebé*."

"*Acá! Acá!*" one of the servants called out as she spied baby Mercedes off to the side of the big soft bed, caught in the folds of hazy white mosquito netting tucked tight around the mattress. Wiggling and squirming, she had tumbled into this hidden place, a safety net, and gone peacefully to sleep.

The netting story became one of Mercedes's favorites. As a little girl she'd ask Gertrude to tell it over and over. She couldn't get enough of hearing how her mother feared losing her. "Mommy, you screamed so loud the servants came running," she'd interrupt. She especially liked hearing how she was found enveloped in a web of whiteness, discovered in a cocoon like a squirmy caterpillar about to become a butterfly. That's what she thought as she grew older and learned of such things. Then that became the part of the story she liked best. Twirling and fluttering her arms, she'd tell Luisa and subsequent maids the tale of her transformation. "*Qué preciosa mariposa*," they would exclaim. That's how Mercedes became known among them as a precious butterfly.

As she expected, not a single picture of a servant. Not one. *Ninguno. Nada*, not even the politically incorrect colonial kind where The Help (Gertrude's term as if they were some sort of prosthetic) are lined in a row, faces as grim as their starched uniforms. Not even a maid in the background by accident. Brown and black bodies always among them, but unexposed, unrevealed, secreted beyond the edges of the photographs.

Not even a snapshot of a *niñera* holding baby Mercedes. You'd expect at least that. Especially since Gertrude credited a Panamanian nanny for keeping Mercedes alive during her first precarious months of life. "You would not be here, dear, if it weren't for her. You barely weighed six pounds."

"The maid took over," she would say with a little pout. "She just took over, wouldn't let me near you. She'd soak you in warm water with all sorts of herbs as if you were a vegetable. I have no idea what they were. And she was always muttering some mumbo-jumbo over you."

But there is a photograph of a little girl dressed in what Mercedes knows—even from this picture faded to a soft brown—was a vivid, striped native costume. The child sits astride a dusty burro amid lush tropical foliage. Her hair is braided in two looped pigtails on either side of her face, fat little *chimbas* with a bow atop each. She could be an indigenous child—until you see her eyes. Clear blue china-doll eyes just like Gertrude's. No blue in this faded brown photograph, not a trace of maternal DNA visible, but it's there.

Who did Mercedes think she was all dressed up in a Peruvian outfit sitting on a donkey and sporting a local hair style? All just for a photo op.

Photo op. She was gussied up for a photo op, but the term didn't exist back then. Coined when Nixon became president. Now newspapers are plastered with photo ops. TV screens and iPads stream, scream photo ops. Fake smiles and fake props. The Bible. Trophy wives galore.

An arm extends. The hand holds the halter of the burro, but the body to which it belongs has been cut away by the right edge of the picture. Only the arm and hand remain. Only what was necessary to hold still the donkey for the safety of the child and the success of the photograph.

The missing body was probably that of a servant. A man, to judge from the rough fabric that sheathes the arm. Perhaps the gardener. Most likely a half-breed descended from a Spaniard who lusted after a native Indios or African housemaid.

Not the same for the African women in Colombia who were mated like animals to white plantation owners to further miscegenation —state ordered mestizaje. Whiteout the African, whitewash over Black by copulation with the Right Sort. They hid deep in the forests but couldn't hide forever. *Expulsión*/expulsion, the ground beneath their feet ripped apart into mines and sugar plantations. *Subyugación*/subjugation.

Not the same for the Shan women in Burma. Soldiers were paid to fornicate with them to dilute that unwanted race. Colonialists in Latin American were eager to screw for free and call it a social obligation. Fornication as an alternative to gas chambers.

Expulsíon. Subyugación. Words easily shifted from language to language by a mere accent or change of consonant. The primary Spanish meaning of violation (*violación*) is rape. Significance is not always so easily shifted.

Subyugación. What was going on in the mind of the man holding the donkey? Did he know he was being cut out of the picture? Did he realize he would become invisible beyond the margins of the shot? What isn't in a photograph is often more important than what is.

Did he even consider that he might be viewed as more than a disembodied arm? And what did he think of the little girl in masquerade? A little girl who lived with her mommy and daddy in a nice big house.

A stack of photographs in the trunk is of that nice big house in Peru: stucco exterior, hallway, living room, dining room, bedrooms. Empty of all inhabitants. Like the scene of a crime, she thinks, cordoned off from the living.

There's her room with its little bed, her parents' room with its big bed subjugated by its ponderous headboard. There's the sitting room without a comfortable place to sit and the dining room dominated by its huge polished table and six heavy chairs. She holds that picture close to the light, squinting. Yes, she can make out the legs of the table and chairs reflected on the gleaming tile floor. Luisa. She would have also been reflected there.

Luisa was the housemaid in Lima. Mercedes wasn't quite five when Luisa disappeared, vanished without even an *adios*. Mommy, where's Luisa? Where's Luisa?

Her timeworn memories are mostly of Luisa's ample, enveloping body with its scent of cinnamon and Murphy's soap and the sing-song rhythm of her soft voice.

But two scenes return again and again with filmic vivacity. She sees a gleaming tile floor—any gleaming tile floor—and there's Luisa on hands and knees waxing the deep, blood-red tiles in their dining room in Lima, squat brown body ribboned with sunshine streaming though slats of a window shutter. Bands of light stroke the hair twisted away from her smooth, broad face. Heavy breasts sway with each stroke of polish. She teases Mercedes as her tiny footprints leave a trace.

"Mira! Mira!. A little ghost has been here. Did you see the little ghost?"

"It's me Luisa. Me! My feet. I'm the little ghost, *soy una pequeña fantasma* . . . whoooo, whoooo."

It's a scene now become so soft and threadbare, Mercedes wonders if it actually occurred or if she's borrowed it from a book or a movie. Or is it totally fabricated out of a longing for such an instance of joy? So much of what happened back then she can't remember, never could remember.

The other scene she knows is all too real, even if it too might be infused with other memories and readings and movies too.

For what it's worth, this is the story she has:

César is driving Luisa home. She always took the jammed blue and yellow bus with chattering people hanging off the sides. Mercedes has no idea what has prompted her father to give Luisa a ride on this particular day—there must be an ulterior motive. Even more unusual, he has brought Mercedes along. He never takes her anywhere.

She's happy to be heading towards the hills, excited to get up close to the little houses of the *pueblos jóvenes* she sees from her bedroom window. Little toy houses, blues and pinks and yellows speckled against the hillside with tiny figures moving about, shapes shifting like in the kaleidoscope her Aunt Lola sent for Christmas. César doesn't seem to notice. It's only later that Mercedes connects the *pueblos jóvenes* with the gun he always carried.

Back then she asks Luisa, "Are the *pueblos* called *jóvenes* because there are a lot of kids there?"

"Oh, *chiquita*, there are many kids, but they are not called *jóvenes* because of the *niños*. It is because of the *pueblos*; they were not there until now when *campesinos*, like me, came to Lima."

But this is before the car ride. No one speaks during that sweltering drive. Certainly not Luisa from the back seat. And certainly not Mercedes. Not a peep out of her when her father is around.

She sits propped up on a cushion in the front seat of César's brand-new car. She looks out over the broad hood so shiny and silvery she has to squint against the glare. They head towards the foothills, the far away ones she can barely see from her window. When they—that is to say César, Mercedes, and Gertrude—drive anywhere it's never in that direction. Actually, the three of them hardly ever drive anywhere together. Family outings are not their thing. Family is not their thing.

As César's car winds up the rutted dirt road, its gleam diminished by the dust it raises, she sees that the houses aren't like toys even if they are very little. Then she sees that they aren't even real houses, just propped up junk—jagged pieces of wood, dirty cardboard, and chunks of rusty metal. Of what has seen from her far-away bedroom window, only the patchwork of colors is the same.

They stop in front of one of the piled-up pieces of stuff. A bit of wood on the front is freshly painted a brilliant aquamarine blue. She's recently learned the word "aquamarine." The "marine" part reminds her of the navy for which she has already formed a dislike— César being a commanding officer on a US submarine—but the "aqua" half is like the water word in Spanish and everything Spanish is good to her. The color itself is pretty. She loves bright colors.

"Qué linda color!" she exclaims to Luisa. Her mother always says something nice about a house when she is visiting

(unlike after she leaves), so Mercedes figures it's the thing to do. And it is a pretty color.

She jumps out of the car, following Luisa as always—daylong everywhere, every waking hour.

César roars, "Get back in the goddamn car! What the fuck are you doing?"

Half-naked children come zigzag running towards her. Scrawny chickens squawk out of their way. A dog barks. She sees César draw his gun from the pocket of the car door. She's scared, not of the kids or of the dog, but of César. What's he going to do? She wants to run, but her feet are weighted, too heavy to lift.

A little boy, a couple of years younger than Mercedes, who just turned five, is naked. His penis waggles as he scampers towards her. She zeroes in on it. She's never seen a penis before—at least not on a human being. More children scramble out of what she realizes is where Luisa lives, her home, if you could call it that. It looks even smaller than Mercedes's bedroom. The floor is just dirt—the same dirt as outside, not shiny tiles like in her house.

César is getting out of the car. Mercedes shocks into a run. She's got to stop him. He's yelling and waving his gun! She needs to get back into the car, crouch down on the floor so the dusty children with almost no clothes can't see her, can't see the embroidered dress their mother has ironed, can't see her white cotton socks and shiny black patent leather shoes. Minutes earlier, she'd been so proud of that outfit. Luisa too had been proud, turning her around, smoothing a crumple in the fabric. *Oh qué bonita mi linda princesita, mi preciosa mariposa.* My beautiful little princess, my precious butterfly, Luisa's repeated endearments day after day. My princess, my butterfly. Mine. Mine! She belongs to Luisa.

As César lurches the car around towards the road, Mercedes wants to push the door open, leap out, rush into Luisa's arms. The car swerves wildly as he accelerates; she can only look back. Luisa is standing in the dusty yard swarming with children, her hands pressed to her cheeks. "*Ay, Dios mio!*" she moans. "*Dios mio!*

"What the fuck is wrong with you!" César is shouting. It is then she realizes she's crying.

"Where's Luisa? Mommy, where's Luisa? Why isn't Luisa here?" she asked the next day and the day after and the one after that.

"She won't be coming to our house anymore," is all Gertrude says. Luisa simply disappeared.

Or was disappeared. Disappeared by César?

≈

On the sidewalk below a woman is speaking in Spanish. Softly. The words are indistinguishable, but the rhythm—the syllable-timed rhythm, vowels never condensed no matter how rapid the speech—is always recognizable. The muted murmur spreads, vibrates in Mercedes's body, a deep tremor like the subway's passing vibration deep beneath her building. In the far away distance another voice cries out in Spanish. *Mira! Mira!* Ghosts banished from photographs leave an impression.

≈ COCKTAIL HOUR

It was the cocktail hour when Mercedes was born in the military hospital. Late afternoon or early evening depending on your perspective and sobriety.

She learned early on she was born during the cocktail hour because Gertrude had told her ad nauseam that the obstetrician had been so drunk he had no idea which end was which. Mercedes could have sprung full-grown from her mother's head like Athena from Zeus and he wouldn't have known the difference. As it was, thanks to a capable nurse, she was bloodily extracted from the same orifice into which half her DNA had been deposited nine months earlier by César.

Not only was the obstetrician face pissed, Gertrude might also have been a bit squiffy (as she would say), pregnancy or no pregnancy (drinking with a bun in the oven wasn't such an issue back then), although that possibility never figured into any of her narrations.

César definitely would have been juiced. He always took his first sip of brandy as he lurched out of bed at 6 a.m. sharp and continued throughout the day. As a little girl, Mercedes would come across small bottles of liquor—like the ones they used to give out for free on airplanes—stashed on shelves behind his military books, underneath papers in his desk drawers, and wedged far into the interior of closets where she sometimes hid from him. Other bottles, the flat kind, were tucked under neatly folded sweaters and rows of boxer shorts ironed by the maids.

César was undoubtedly joining neighbors for the cocktail hour at the time Gertrude was in labor. Perhaps the obstetrician himself was there when he got the call to bring Mercedes into the world. Her parents always joined people for cocktails. The men in their sharply pressed outfits would stand in one part of the room chortling off-color jokes. Mercedes still recalls the tart, musky aroma of Jack Daniels and cheese canapés released with every guffaw. César's breath, however, issuing from below his sharp pencil mustache, was mint-fresh as he sipped a glass of water. A closet alcoholic, he rarely drank in public and never appeared to be drunk, but he was never cold sober.

It was the year Mercedes turned six that cocktail time acquired a more immediate symbolic status as it entered the realm of Psychological Trauma. César had been relocated to Cuba. Shortly after the move and inexplicably no longer in the navy, he was at home. It was then that Mercedes was called on to play a part during the cocktail hour. A maid would be sent to fetch her from where she cowered in her bedroom, hoping that, for once, César would forget her existence. He never did, at least not during those gatherings. She would be inescapably, unavoidably, inevitably trotted out among the assembled guests.

In the living room men would be standing in clusters, ice cubes clinking as amber-colored drinks jostled in their beefy hands. César would call attention to her panties, their outlines visible beneath the white gauzy dolly dress he bought specifically for Mercedes' evening dress up.

In 2007 the artist Karen LaMonte forged a child's dress out of thick glass tinged blue-gray. Transparency on the threshold of the opaque. A little over a foot high it stands upright and empty. Short sleeves angle sideways as if the dress were on a hanger. An enormous bow sits beneath a high collar. Ruffles are in immobile flutter at the hip. A picture of this frock has been tacked on Mercedes' bulletin board for years.

Glass can wound when shattered, she thinks. The time has come to pull out the push pins, take the picture out of sight.

"Don't we have a modest little lady. I wonder what she's hiding under there." César's melodious voice ever so smooth. He had a lovely voice, seductive, a Frank Sinatra crooner's voice.

Did the men chuckle politely? Laugh outright? Mercedes remembers only the grip of César's hand on her arm and the navy blue and blood red of the rug beneath her, at its center a mandala of expanding zigzags outlined in black. If she thought hard enough in Spanish . . . *el tapete, tapete, el tapete* . . . and stared long enough, the rug would begin to shift, sway, elevate, envelop her in its softness.

We all have billions of electrons in our bodies along with iron and other elements. Changes in such matter are minimal even after death. *For a significant number of electrons to leave the body ... [they would have to be] forcefully stripped away, e.g. by an electric field applied from outside. ... You could arrange for this to happen by wrapping the body in plastic wrap and dragging it over a wool carpet ...* (Carl Smotricz, *Quora*). Could willing oneself to disappear into a carpet change a body count of electrons? The mind does strange things.

And the women? The women decorously sipped their whiskies, perched on sofas and armchairs, padded shoulders angled towards one another, well-groomed legs demurely crossed—for the first drink. When Mercedes appeared, they'd pause in their discussion of bridge hands and of their satisfaction or dissatisfaction with the local servants. Mercedes assumed that was their conversation, because that's all they ever talked about, besides the difficulty of finding a good hairdresser.

Gertrude? She was mute. She never referred to Mercedes's presence at cocktail time during or afterwards.

"Oh, I see two little mosquito bites on your chest," César would continue. "What have you been up to, little girl, that you got pricked?"

The double entendre was beyond Mercedes's comprehension then, but she knew it was a dirty joke. Jokes having to do with vaginas were César's favorite stock in trade. A woman was petting her Chihuahua . . . Mercedes doesn't remember more, probably because she never understood the punch line. She didn't even know what a Chihuahua was.

But the one about the parrot that squawked obsceni-ties—that joke, oh yes, she's never forgotten that one. The bird's throat was slit, traumatically fissured, and it was dumped into a toilet. A very fat, menstruating woman entered the bathroom and seated herself on the porcelain throne (César's term, when he didn't call it the crapper or the can). The parrot looked up and said, if she can live with that bloody slit, I can live with mine. Glasses clinked. Men laughed. The women continued their chatter, pretending not to have heard.

Later César would sneak into Mercedes's bedroom, pull her onto his lap, pinch her nipples hard under her nightie. Pushing her bony little buttocks tight against the lump in his pants, he'd slip the panties she insisted on wearing to bed aside from her crotch. She'd smell the whiskey panting of his breath on her neck, feel the heat of it and the scratch of his mustache as he pressed his lips against her bare flesh. Then came the jab of his finger, his trigger finger, into where it hurt. When she cried out he put his free hand over her mouth, flattened her onto her bed, and rocked himself against her hard, hard, hard until, with a groan, he rushed to the bathroom. She'd hear the toilet flushing and think of the parrot, gurgling in the bowl, its throat slashed.

"This is our little secret," César would say. "Don't you dare tell. Something very, very bad will happen if you tell. Our secret. Remember, it's our secret."

Mercedes had every good cause to believe something very bad would happen if she told. César talked constantly about killing—killing people. He never told stories about blasting submarines and their crews to bits or about anyone he killed at sea or on land. He ranted about people he was *going* to kill. If that son of a bitch ever comes near me again with that so-and-so, I swear I'll kill him . . . Goddamnit, if he does that one more time I'll kill the little prick.

She'd seen César explode over nothing, his face mottled red like a slab of salami. One time it was when the fringes of a carpet weren't combed to his liking. The maids were ordered to comb the fringes every day. Perhaps they had been perfectly aligned, but someone had nudged them askew in an unpardonable careless saunter across the room. Mercedes knew she wasn't the culprit. She was super careful not to step on the fringes, avoiding them like superstitious children or compulsive elders avoid cracks on a sidewalk.

"*Torcido!*" César had screamed at the maid. "*Mira! Mira!* A fucking mess! *Torcido! Torcido!* Crooked! *Mira! Mira!* A fucking mess! *Qué desorden"!* he'd yelled in an escalating volume of repetitious rage.

Also on Mercedes bulletin board: pictures of the artist Ewa Kuryluk's nude body drawn in acrylic and felt-tip pens onto crumpled white cloth. Her fragmented and torqued hands, arms, breasts, and legs partially disappear into jagged folds of scrunched cotton skins. Her face is severed, grotesque, maimed. Threats are drawn onto her body: a knife poised against her belly, a syringe aimed at her navel, pins and nails here and there piercing her flesh. Why are you doing this to yourself? Ewa asked. She titled one series "Interrogation."

Why am I doing this to myself? Mercedes asks. Why? Was her story of the little girl whose severed body pieces were scattered throughout the world about pain and dispersal as well as about hope? She pulls out the tacks that anchor Ewa's pictures in place. Mutilated body parts drift down to her desk. She folds them tightly away in the back of a drawer. Maybe she'll throw them away next week.

Torcido! Crooked! *Mira! Mira!* A fucking mess! *Qué desorden!*

≈ INMACULADA

Inmaculada was the cook when the family moved to Cuba. Mercedes spent all possible waking hours in the kitchen, the safest room in the house. She never could be sure when César might show up. His was not a nine-to-five, I'm-home-honey job. When he was in the navy he'd be gone for weeks and then without warning come striding through the door—striding being his only mode of ambulation, even when he'd been drinking, which was always. Mercedes can't imagine César ever strolling, sauntering, ambling along, tiptoeing, or even running, for that matter. No, his was always a manly, chest to the wind, military advance: stride, stride, stride. Hup. Hup. Hup. One. Two. Three. In Cuba and no longer in the navy, his strident comings and goings were constant and even more unpredictable. But he never set foot in the kitchen. Never. *Jamás.* Which is partly why the kitchen became the center of Mercedes's life.

She loved the gaudy vibrancy of the multicolored floor and wall tiles, the shiny hanging pots, the fruits and vegetables scattered among dishrags—the kaleidoscope of shapes and colors a contrast to the somber beige elegance of the rest of the house. The kitchen was the only disorderly room in a house where everything had to be perfectly shipshape. Shipshape. One of César's favorite words. Nothing could be out of place, even for an instant. Yet, the kitchen had its own order. Like a kaleidoscope, its fragments came together to form distinctive shifting harmonies.

All this, yes, but it was mainly because of Inmaculada that Mercedes spent much of her time in the kitchen. She was there the minute she heard the slap, slap of Inmaculada's rope sandals. Was there to see her set them out on the broad ledge of the back patio's stucco wall so they wouldn't get messed up by chickens that fluttered and clucked and babies that crawled and toddled and babbled. Once inside, Inmaculada always went barefoot (one among the many things César would not have tolerated). She had huge black feet, calloused and gray at the edges, strong and beautiful like her hands. Mercedes knew Inmaculada would protect her if César violated her sanctuary with his presence. The servants knew something was going on between her and César. *Ay, pobrecita, pequeña pobrecita.* Poor little one, they'd mutter.

There were big knives in the kitchen. The biggest of all was the cleaver Inmaculada used to slice off the heads of the chickens she carried home squawking and flapping from market. With one hand she'd grab a chicken's head, stretch its neck taut across the chopping block, and, with the other, whack the head off in a single, strong swing of the cleaver. The hen behaved just like a chicken with its head cut off—which it was—running in fluttery zigzags all over the little patio. Inmaculada was always crouched and ready to seize the headless fowl and catch the blood that spurted from its neck into a dented tin cup. Triumphantly blood-splattered and sticky with feathers, she would drink it with gusto, hot from the source.

"Makes me strong," she'd declare. "*Muy fuerte, fuertissima.*"

And she was strong. Big and strong and thickly odorous of onions, garlic, rice, black beans, and her warm black fleshiness. Comforting, blessedly comforting.

Mercedes was never invited to share Inmaculada's bloody beverage, but had she been, she would have accepted. Long before learning about the white woman in Tennessee who drank the blood of her black lover to be counted as black so she could legally marry her man, Mercedes felt that sharing the warm red elixir from Inmaculada's tin cup would relate them by blood.

Inmaculada's name had puzzled Mercedes. She knew *inmaculada* meant immaculate. Not possible to live with César, even sporadically, without learning that word early on. Immaculate! Must be immaculate! What she couldn't understand was why Inmaculada—her apron gorgeously besplattered,

its colors changing according to whatever she was preparing—
why *she* was named Inmaculada.

For a long time she hesitated to ask. Gertrude had taught
her it was rude to ask people about matters pertaining to their
private lives. ("Pertaining" was one of the words that Gertrude,
a farm girl who had not gone to college, had assembled. Words
as carefully selected as her elegant wardrobe and Chanel No.5
perfume.)

Inmaculada was downright filthy according to
Gertrude's standards. As for César, he'd have been positively
apoplectic if he'd caught sight of her big apron smeared with
dabs of blood, green and purple streaks of vegetables, and ripe
red tomato drips mixed with orange globs of papayas. Abstract
painting *avant la lettre*. Not that César would have tolerated the
sight of abstract paintings either.

Come to think of it, Inmaculada's apron was a form of
art, an expression of her pleasure in getting down and dirty with
the abundance of food in their home, a contrast to the meager
supply of victuals in her own home. She sang and swayed as
her big hands scooped black seeds from the orange belly of a
papaya or plunged into the deep innards of a chicken, pulling
out pink guts and blue gizzards.

But a name was a public word, Mercedes reasoned,
trumping the dictate that cleanliness was a personal matter. So
one day she went ahead and asked.

"*Oh preciosa cariña,*" Inmaculada said, "I'm named after the *Santa Virgin Maria*, holy mother of *Jésus Cristo.*"

That was the first Mercedes had heard of the Virgin Mary's cleanliness. But she already knew that people had dangerous secrets.

One secret was the maids' children in the walled, back patio. César called them "little black bastards." For him, all native children were "little bastards." It didn't take much to figure out that none of them would ever have been allowed in his house. Even as a child, Mercedes knew that, at the very least, the offending mother would be fired on the spot if César discovered her baby. They all held their breath when his hup-hup footsteps sounded nearby, fearful that for once he might venture into that distant part of the house. Or that he might hear the babies' gurgles and cries, though hardly perceptible blended with the neighborhood sounds of squalling children on the street, rumbling cars, yapping dogs, blasts from the occasional radio, and the immediate kitchen cacophony of squawking chickens, sizzling foods, knives on chopping boards, chatter and humming and singing of the maids.

Gertrude also mostly avoided the kitchen. For one, knowing only three or four words of Spanish, she relied on her daughter for all communications with the cook as well as with the other maids. She probably figured that babies were stashed in the patio from time to time, but as long as she didn't have to see them or admit hearing them, she could feign ignorance.

Her only sign of recognition of the *niños* out back was to tell Mercedes that it was never a good idea to get too close to local children.

"They look like they all have dreadful diseases," she would say with a grimace that took her glamorous blonde looks down a peg or two.

Mercedes loved the babies—living toys! They smiled back at her, squeezed her fingers and kicked their scrawny little legs against her belly when she held them. That they cried, farted, pissed, shat, and spit up was all part of being with them. In that back patio world of children and mothers, bodies were accepted in the fullness of their nature. Bodily overflows were casually wiped away with a damp cloth. Mercedes only fully registered that the babies were live human beings when little Carlita didn't show up for several weeks. She'd been the one most often crawling around in the back patio.

"Where is she?" she asked Inmaculada.

"She was called to heaven to be with God and Jesus and all the angels."

"She's dead!" Mercedes wailed, angry at Carlita for not staying alive and at being fed such a line.

Despite exposure to the servants' fervent Catholicism, Mercedes didn't believe in heaven or angels. Even Santa Claus was suspect. Proof of his having been around was dubious. And there were never presents from God or saints or angels. Nothing from *them* in her Christmas stocking, a fat, wooly, red lump propped on a wooden chair in front of an array of bougainvillea, not hanging by the fireplace like the ones on the holiday cards from Rhode Island that Granz and Gramps sent every year.

Children died. Mercedes will have several so there will always be an extra.

≈ MELISSA

There would have been Melissa, the forever unborn.

Mercedes became pregnant her second year with Enrico in Barcelona. They both agreed it wasn't the right time for a baby. They were living on the proverbial shoestring and the shoestring was primarily made up of Mercedes' freelance translating. The possibility of Enrico taking on more of his own translating was never raised. And finding a regular job was out of the question for a poet, he insisted.

The abortion, illegal, had been excruciating and bloody. The pain from the butchery of her womb eventually subsided, the bleeding gradually diminished. What didn't go away was the anguish of being told she would never be able to have children. Several years after the abortion, her yearning for a child more acute, Mercedes broached the idea of adopting. Three or four, a mix of boys and girls would be great. Or even just one. Maybe, was all Enrico would say. She dropped the subject, convinced he'd change his mind in time. In good time when he'd become a successful writer, when they had more money, a bigger home. When, when, when. Never, she now realizes. Perhaps she'd insisted too often, and that was why he'd walked out without a word of explanation.

From the beginning, Mercedes had named the unborn child: Melissa. This she never revealed to anyone, certainly not Enrico. Despite the absence of proof, she was sure the baby was a girl. The little ghost. *La pequeña fantasma.* She'd calculated that February 3rd would have been Melissa's birthday. Born under the sign of Aquarius, she would have been affectionate, creative, a seeker of truth—if one believes in astrology. In this case, Mercedes believes.

The ghost of Melissa would not have haunted Mercedes had there been other children. Hers is not a prolonged mourning for that unborn being, but for those who were never conceived or adopted afterwards, those who never had a name. Melissa became the invisible, encompassing presence of an ongoing absence of motherhood, the container for that absence.

Especially in February, Mercedes has kept track of her unborn: She'd be a year old and starting to walk on chubby legs, babbling a word or two. *Mamá.* She'd call me *Mamá.* She'd be in kindergarten. First grade. Graduating from high school. College. She'd have children of her own and I'd be a grand-mother, an *abuela.*

Did Frieda Kahlo, in pain her entire life from a tram crash, count the years of her miscarried baby, knowing she would never be able to bear another child? She wrote her be-loved *Doctorcito* twelve days after the loss. *I cried a lot, but it's over, there is nothing else that can be done except to bear it.* She bore it by painting violent, bloody renditions of her shattered, gutted body, her agony hung out on museum walls for the world to see.

Mercedes bore it in different ways. Returning to New York empty-wombed and alone, she was fiercely promiscuous. Had she hoped for a miraculous pregnancy despite her doctors' insistence it was not possible? After she turned fifty she was celibate, exhausted by the years of angry, vigorous sex designed to reduce men to helpless moaning orgasms.

It was then, womb and heart shattered, that the translating that had been merely work, became a refuge, an addiction, a drug of choice. Lost in the concatenations of words, their vibrations from morpheme to morpheme, language to language, sentence to sentence, swimming toward *the confluence where the dissimilar is one* (Fady Joudah), she became other than her incongruous self, her dissimilar made one. Deep into the words and thoughts and lives of others her piecemeal self was made whole, her anger quieted.

She owed her stellar reputation to her ability to mute— suppress? cancel? annihilate?—her own voice, her very being, in the service of an author's. Friends told her that her emails read differently according to whom she was translating.

She was often asked why she became a translator. I was born into it, she'd say, born in Panama, one long isthmus connecting different countries. Born isthmian. (That last part never went over well. She should have dropped it, but she was in love with the image and the word, a word so close to being a lisp.) She would quickly segue into how, when she was just a tiny tot, she was her mother's interpreter. And how, as soon as she could read, her mother would mark recipes in the *Fanny Farmer* cookbook and send her off to the kitchen to translate them.

At first she'd been proud to be Mommy's little helper, proud she could speak two languages like papa César. It was fun to convey the day's menus, thumbing through the tattered, splotched cookbook, making up silly words, drawing pictures of yellow squashes and red peppers and chickens and cows. But it wasn't all fun and games when she had to tell the maids to scrub *caca* from the toilets, wash the floors, shake out the rugs, and carefully dust the antiques. As she became more attached to the servants, she was increasingly mortified by having to tell them when Gertrude was displeased with the fold of a sheet on a bed, an overcooked vegetable, a table not polished to a shine that reflected Gertrude's face as she leaned over to inspect it.

Back then she translated—interpreted is more apt for the spoken word—back and forth from English to Spanish. Subsequently, in her professional work, her translations have been mostly from Spanish into English, the language she's been speaking much of her adult life.

She worries about "doing violence" to the original as one translator describes the process. Or, as another writes, "domesticating the original" by moving words and sentence clauses around to make it easier for a reader to understand, subtleties be damned. And changing an object to something familiar to the reader's culture, often food. No. No. No. Not if she can help it. *Patatas bravas*, a dish known only to those who frequent tapas bars, she kept in Spanish the one time it came up. Brave potatoes! Boiled potatoes with sauce. No! A culinary insult. A betrayal.

She didn't like English as a child. Gertrude spoke English, only English, rigid, tense English. Spanish was the warmth and safety of the maids who cared for her. But Spanish was also César, military order and violence.

So not only was there a divide between Spanish and English but, for Mercedes, also a rift within Spanish itself. Enveloped in the spread and flow of Spanish with the maids, assailed by César's rages, or subjected to Gertrude's uptight English, Mercedes was three different little girls.

Did Katie, her father Japanese and mother American, feel like two little girls in one body? Maybe not. Her parents were a steadfast unit, similar despite cultural differences.

Who are you going to sleep with? Katie had asked when Mercedes once spent the night in their rambling Maine house. Mommy sleeps with Daddy and I sleep with my cat.

I'm sleeping by myself.

You need a lovey, Katie had said, and gave her the fuzzy, pink rhinoceros that still flops, threadbare, on Mercedes' bed.

She wells up thinking of the child, plump and rosy. And of Katie's mother, Susan, her scarred chest festooned with tattooed roses after a double mastectomy. Roses that bloomed for three years until the underlying roots of disease spread to parts that could not be uprooted or planted over. Susan wasn't able to see her child grow into an adult.

So many immigrant families never see their children grow up. And now, in the midst of the deadly pandemic, the Department of Homeland Security is presenting families, even breastfeeding mothers, with a horrific, wrenching choice: separate from your children or stay together in jail indefinitely where the Virus runs rampant.

A photo of a crying little boy haunts Mercedes. Wearing an oversized red t-shirt he clings to his mother's thigh, barely able to get his arms around its solid fullness. The mother's head is cut off by the frame, her anger and grief not represented.

Forty-three. Melissa would be forty-three now. Might she be living nearby? With children? What would she say about her mother going back to the lands of her childhood? Would Mercedes even consider it if she had grandchildren?

But she doesn't.

≈ HOME SCHOOLING

After the family moved to Cuba, Gertrude began home schooling her daughter. Mercedes was seven and had had no formal education during the relocations from Panama to Peru. It wasn't that Gertrude believed in home schooling; there was not a single slot available at the American school and she certainly wasn't about to send a daughter of hers to a Cuban one. Lord knows what heathen ideas she might pick up, not to mention diseases. (Gertrude was obsessed with diseases when abroad, but not back in the USA.)

Well, she'd certainly be obsessed if she were alive now, this deadly Virus running rampant in her sanitized homeland. Probably die from the Virus in the nursing home. How … nice … to … see … you her last gasp as doctors came to intubate her?

Every week a Calvert System packet wrapped in well-travelled brown paper tied with a coarse brown string would arrive. Gertrude and Mercedes would "repair" to César's study. (The use of "repair" in conjunction with locomotion was another one of Gertrude's I-am-a-sophisticated-woman words.)

It was only for the Calvert System lessons that either of them, with César's permission, set foot in his inner sanctum. A dark place shuttered off from the bright sunny house, its centerpiece was an enormous mahogany desk with a matching straight-back chair. On the desk, sheathed in a leather case, was a nautical ruler that Mercedes was forbidden to take out of its scabbard. Above the desk hung a large, massively framed, black and white photograph of the *Foxtrot*, the submarine on which César had served. A silly name, Mercedes thought, even before she learned it was a dance.

It wasn't the *Foxtrot* picture, but the clock set solidly be-low it that commanded most of Mercedes' attention as it ticked off the two hours of her daily lessons. A brass Chelsea Ships Bell Clock from the 1920s, it had been a present from his father when César had graduated from the naval academy. César said it was the Rolls Royce of marine instruments. Mercedes didn't know what a Rolls Royce was, but, from César's intonation, she figured it meant the clock was very special. She was convinced its hands dragged behind the actual progression of time. Gertrude was undoubtedly of the same opinion.

A tide of sympathy edges its way into Mercedes when she recalls how nervous Gertrude became when it was time for the lessons. Even as a seven-year-old, Mercedes knew her mother was afraid of her, afraid of the odd child she had inadvertently spawned who, aside from china-doll blue eyes, bore no resemblance to her in body or mind. But Gertrude was possessed by a fierce Yankee determination to do her duty. And many of her friends, all Americans stoically enduring their expatriation, were also educating their children according to the Calvert system.

At the end of every week there was a test. Mercedes would write the answers and Gertrude would check them against those provided by the teacher's book. Mercedes thought the questions absurdly easy. There must be a trick, she reasoned. She let her imagination—even as a child she was inclined to far-flung associative configurations—delve for hidden agendas. Every week she failed every test.

Now Mercedes wonders: Are there remnants of the Calvert System in the trunk? Evidence? Testimony?

What's this? A penciled draft of a letter. (Gertrude always drafted letters that she later copied in her elegant, slanted cursive.) *My daughter cannot complete the simplest Calvert System test which leads me to believe she is somewhat retarded, although she seems almost normal in most aspects of her behavior.*

Retarded! Almost normal! Most aspects! What the fuck! My God, my mother thought I was a freak! Retarded? I'd taught myself to read.

Mercedes could read by the time she was four. Not that Gertrude knew. She only found out on a visit to Connecticut, when Aunt Lola, who always knew more about her niece than her own mother did, exclaimed, "Mercedes can read! How precocious."

According to Aunt Lola's telling of the story, Gertrude immediately proclaimed, "That's not possible. No one has taught her to read. You're confusing her with some other child." Mercedes is sure she'd replied with conviction. Like many insecure people, Gertrude was always dead certain of any and all of her opinions.

Mercedes flips Gertrude's letter back to see the response clipped beneath it. Natalie Steward of the Calvert System emphatically assures Gertrude that her daughter is not in the least retarded, but, in fact, advanced for her age. She strongly suggests home instruction be discontinued and Mercedes be put in a school where her intelligence will be recognized and cultivated. Or at least put in in the hands of an experienced tutor.

Wow! Gertrude who never saved anything, had preserved these letters to her dying day. All those years she kept them with her. How desperate and bewildered she must have been. Natalie pulled no punches: Gertrude was not fit to educate her daughter. Raised on a farm, only a rural high school education, she'd failed as a teacher of a mere child. And as a mother who didn't understand her own daughter. Failures held in check by elegant penmanship and fancy words. Shall we repair to the study …

Had Gertrude saved the letters for Mercedes to discover? A post-mortem apology? Was it her fault that she was totally devoid of imagination or curiosity? That she had to memorize fancy words to seem smart?

Curiosity: related to the Latin *cura*, meaning "care." Things matter. Take care. *Te cuides.* The last words Inmaculada whispered in Mercedes' ear as she wrapped her belly close in big, strong arms. *Te cuides mi preciosa mariposa, te cuides.* Take care my precious butterfly, take care.

Mercedes puts the letters aside to save. Take care. Why this anger against the dead? Why is she doing this to herself? Let it go.

Let go her anger towards the living too? Cool her rage over greedy politicians and other fat cats who care only for themselves? Police who kill when they should protect. No. Not them. She's furious and she should be, needs to be. Lives are at stake. All over the world people are homeless, hungry, dying because of the vicious, hateful, destructive corruption of those who wield power over the vulnerable and defenseless.

Gertrude was not evil. She was simply ignorant, oblivious, and insecure.

≈ THE SCRAPBOOK

The scrapbook. Mercedes rummages again through the trunk looking for the scrapbook. It's not there. Gertrude didn't save it. Why didn't she save it? Did she lose it? Throw it away? How could she!

She was never into hoarding mementoes. No saved postcards, no crayon drawings by little Mercedes in Gertrude's desk drawers. Not that she lived in a Zen present or that she ascribed to a robust *carpe diem*. Gertrude lived in the anxiety of the next moment. Could never invest herself fully in The Now. But get rid of the scrapbook! Evidence of the most precious, special time Mercedes had spent with her as a child. Evidence of Gertrude's unique, unwitting home schooling.

Mercedes is struck by a stab of the old, familiar anger.

The scrapbook was put together shortly after the family relocated to Cuba. Mercedes was out walking accompanied by a maid, Maria-Rosa it was, when a gust of wind blew slivers of metal from a construction site into her eyes. She was rushed to a hospital where it took over an hour for each minuscule scrap to be tweezed out. Strapped tight to the operating surface, her eyelids were clamped open. She felt no pain, but screamed every time the shiny surgical instruments approached her face. Afterwards her eyes were bandaged for what might have been only a week, but seemed a long, long time.

While Mercedes was in a state of blindness, Gertrude made her a scrapbook of pictures cut from a copy of LIFE magazine, one of the many Aunt Lola regularly forwarded.

As she snipped and pasted by her daughter's side Gertrude described the pictures, her words scented by wafts of her signature Chanel No. 5. "A lovely woman in a beautiful white crochet hat and gloves. A sweet doggie. And here is a picture of a movie set! There's a sofa and flowers and an actor standing in the middle and my goodness gracious lots of huge cameras everywhere and microphones hanging down and lots of men gathered all around. In this other picture a man is measuring the distance between a camera and the actor's nose. Can you imagine that! I'd love to go to Hollywood someday."

Mercedes had never seen a movie, but as Gertrude recounted those she'd seen—*Panama Lady* was a favorite—Mercedes decided she very much wanted to go to the movies as soon as she could. "Take me, Mommy, take me to a movie when I can see again."

Over the next days, Gertrude continued telling Mercedes about pictures of adorable little girls with their beautiful mothers, more cute doggies and a kitty cat too, a racehorse, a smiling man in an elegant suit, and other very handsome men. All smiling. They're all so handsome, she'd exclaim. So handsome!

And food, lots of pictures of food: Armour ham, Snider chili sauce, Green Giant canned peas, Libby pineapples, Pep-o-Mint lifesavers, Heinz tomato soup. "I studied home economics in high school," Gertrude informed Mercedes. "I learned everything about a proper diet."

For cleanup after all the food (very important), there were pictures of Palmolive soap, Ipana toothpaste, Prolon toothbrushes, and Listerine mouthwash. To get away from it all was Samsonite luggage. "The kind we use, dear, when we go home to Gramps and Granz in Rhode Island." A woman at a Royal typewriter set Gertrude to reminiscing about her time at Katie Gibbs secretarial school in Providence.

"Oh, and here are ninety-nine New York debutantes dancing at the Waldorf, all of them gorgeous."

"What are debutantes?" Mercedes asked. "And what's the Waldorf?"

"Rich young girls being shown off," Gertrude replied. "I was never one of them. The Waldorf is a fancy place, a hotel where people go to show off."

"You will see all of this once the bandages are removed," Gertrude would repeat as she snipped and glued reminiscences and longings. When her eyes were finally unwrapped, Mercedes recognized every one of the pictures.

≈

No scrapbook. But a blue envelope—no name no address—is wedged at the edge of the trunk. One of the items Mercedes had slipped in years ago, cracking the lid open just a sliver. She tugs it out. Opens it.

Happy Birthday

Sadie

May 31st

Many happy returns

of the day

With much <u>much</u> love

Mother

"Your Mom"

May 31st was Gertrude's birthday! She must have already been struggling through the fog of dementia. She was trying, trying hard to remember her daughter. Mother. Your Mom. Had she been trying all along? Much *much* love. Yet the date was her own birthday, not her daughter's. She had joined the two of them at the date.

The LIFE magazine Gertrude cut up to make Mercedes' scrapbook isn't in the trunk. Why would it be? Mercedes logs on to the internet. What year would that have been? 1946? Summertime? After an hour of scrolling she finds the issue. Yes, the pictures she remembers are there: Prolon toothbrush, debutants, Hollywood set... And lots of pictures her mother never included in her narrations and pastings: so many ads for booze and cigarettes of all varieties. And pictures of war. Not a single one of those made it into the scrapbook. Not even the handsome soldier standing at attention.

Gertrude, a military wife, drank and smoked back then.

Her mother—her clueless, insensitive mother—was trying to give her good memories, memories of movies and clothes and foods saved for when she could see again. Trying to give her a future as yet unseen. Memories for a future. In her own way, misguided as it may have been, Gertrude was trying to educate her daughter to a world of material products and unfulfilled yearnings. And a cautionary lesson too: The Waldorf, a fancy place where people go to show off.

Was this an attempt to protect her daughter from the hurt of exclusion that was always with Gertrude, a hurt that no designer clothes and acquired vocabulary could cover?

≈ FUZO

It was the cook Inmaculada who rushed to gather her in her arms when Fuzo was killed. He was a small mutt of an indeterminate brown, one of the many street dogs that were common even in their upscale neighborhood in Havana, nameless until Mercedes baptized him with a flick of water. Inmaculada told her that if someone died without being baptized he couldn't go to heaven. All of Inmaculada's children were baptized as soon as they were born. That's why Inmaculada knew that when one of her babies died, she'd gone to heaven. Mercedes wasn't sure she believed in heaven, but she wasn't taking any chances.

Fuzo began hanging out around the back of their house, not because he'd been baptized, but because Mercedes, in secret acts of defiance, would sneak out to pet him and feed him tidbits from the kitchen.

"Don't you ever, ever go near those dogs. They're horridly filthy and they all have fleas," Gertrude admonished. César would mutter, "Damn mutts. Worse than rats. Why the fuck doesn't Socarrás get rid of them. Useless government."

Neither was Mercedes allowed to be friendly with César's prized Dobermans, Brutus and Portia. Doberman Pinschers. (French *pincer*: to grip, pinch.) Sleek and muscled with long, verifiable pedigrees, fierce objects of César's fierce pride trained to guard his property and never allowed inside the house. "The dogs are not damn toys, Mercedes. They're here to protect us. Don't ruin them."

When Mercedes was sure César had gone out she'd run her hand softly along their backs. She renamed them Gus and Lucy. Friendlier names, she thought, even before she learned that Brutus was a murderer and Portia a suicide. Gus … Lucy, she'd whisper into the pink lining of their ears. Gus. Lucy. Good dog. Good dog. Perhaps that was why, sensing how Mercedes doted on Fuzo, the Dobermans ignored the little mutt who, however, was careful not to push his luck.

Despite his life on the street, Fuzo was an irrepressibly joyous creature. The slightest pat on the head sent his whole body waggling with delight. He happily tolerated the frequent scrubbings and dowsings of soap and water Mercedes subjected him to in hopes that if Gertrude saw him at least *she* would accept him, seeing how clean he was.

The servants were well aware of the time Mercedes was spending with Fuzo in the back ally and careful never to mention it to her parents, especially César. They would cover for her when either one happened to call her. *Aquí, aquí en cocina.* She's in the kitchen, they'd say, and hurriedly drag her inside. Despite their caution and despite the fact that César never ventured to the back of the house where the kitchen and servants' quarters were located, the day came when he discovered what Mercedes had been up to.

"Come out of the house. Out here in front," César commanded. "Call that damn dog."

Mercedes knew the "damn dog" he was yelling about wasn't Brutus or Portia. She obeyed. Fuzo, in turn, obeyed when she called him and came bouncing around from the back, his pink tongue lolling out from the nicotine colored fur around his muzzle.

"Hold him by the scruff of his neck."

Fuzo looked up at her trustingly as she patted his head.

"I said, hold the mutt by the scruff of its neck."

"Why?" The word erupted in a wail before Mercedes realized the sound she'd emitted.

César's eyes narrowed, his handsome face livid and distorted.

"Who the hell do you think you are to question my orders. Insubordinate brat."

Her whole body shaking, Mercedes crouched and clasped the coarse fur at the base of Fuzo's skull. It was over in an instant. She didn't even see César draw his gun. One shot to the head.

César turned his back and marched off, leaving Mercedes crumpled beside Fuzo's body. Blood trickled from his mouth onto the hand that cradled his limp head. A passerby glanced at the little girl crying over her dog but didn't intervene. César had a reputation in the neighborhood: a man not to be messed with. *No te metas con él, ah no.*

Mercedes became terrified she would be shot in the head if she didn't instantly obey her father, or even if he so much as imagined she hadn't obeyed. When she confessed her fear to Inmaculada she was assured that God would protect her.

"Why didn't God protect Fuzo?" Mercedes sobbed.

"Because God was *muy ocupado*—very, very busy— protecting you, just the way he saved the boy Isaac in the Bible. Remember?"

The big cleaver Inmaculada used to chop the heads off the chickens raised on high, Inmaculada swooped down towards an imaginary Isaac, stopping theatrically mid-swing as the hand of God prevented Abraham from killing his son. Mercedes knew Inmaculada would never kill any of her children, God or no God. But César, oh yes, he might hack Mercedes's head off even if God came along.

After Fuzo was shot Mercedes' screams pierced the household as she woke from the same nightmare again and again: César was after her with a gun. She'd locked herself in a bathroom. She wanted to slide into a tub of warm water but she was covered in blood and would be punished if she bloodied the waters.

It wasn't long before she was sent away to live with Granz and Gramps in Rhode Island. Oblivious to her daughter as she was, Gertrude realized something must be done to protect her from César. Yet Gertrude stayed in Havana. Stayed another two years until she fled and joined her daughter.

When Gertrude made the final break, she snuck out of Havana in secret. Only when there were more than a thousand miles between her and César did she write to say she wasn't coming back. No, she wasn't even the one who wrote. She had César's brother, Uncle Joe, as sweet as César was hateful, write.

≈ PANAMA LADY

A long forgotten memory: Gertrude alone in her bedroom in Havana. Morning sun floods the room, sparkles disheveled blond hair, slithers down a back to naked buttocks swaying to a silent beat beneath a transparent lacy slip. Mercedes backs silently away from the half-open door.

Something Granz said decades past edges into Mercedes's reminiscence. "Gertrude was a wild one when she was young. Not just her kooky sister but, oh my goodness, Gertrude too." A softness at odds with Granz's usual assertive speech came into her voice. "Such crazy girls they were. Full of mischief, my girls. Gertrude had a gang of friends and they'd run all over the place. She was very popular, your mother was." A pause. "César snuffed the life out of her."

Gertrude crazy and wild? The woman Mercedes remembers wearing a thick girdle every day, even at breakfast? Gertrude, hair sprayed into a helmet as hard and impenetrable as theft-resistant packaging? Gertrude, hair and butt firmly under control, a crazy wild teenager?

In that sunlit room, had she been dancing to the forbidden salsa, flamenco, tango, and merengue music that echoed along the marble halls of the lavish Hotel Nacional? Rhythms heard from a distance when Gertrude and César would go to the Nacional. But never to dance. César refused to attend dance parties anywhere. If they went to the Nacional it was to hear Frank Sinatra when he was in town, the only form of entertainment acceptable to César, probably because his singing voice was eerily close to Sinatra's.

Alone in her room was Gertrude dancing with Al Capone? Or another one of the mafia? One among the mob that had taken over the entire sixth floor of the Nacional for a summit meeting?

"Who are they?" Mercedes wanted to know having eavesdropped on Gertrude and her friends bandying about strange names—Lucky Luciano, Santo Trafficante Jr., Moe Dalitz, and the like—words tumbling fast, voices high pitched, hands fluttering over crustless cucumber sandwiches.

"Very bad men, crooks. Go to your room," was all Gertrude had said, sparkly eyed and flushed, the thrill of Lucky and Santo and Moe still in her voice.

Gertrude wore long-sleeved blouses for a month after she came home to Rhode Island. She refused to go to the beach. Despite her precautions, Mercedes spied purple splotches on her mother's arms and once, as she walked in on her mother un-dressing, violet and green islands on her stomach, a geography of assault. What was that about? What had she done? Sneaked off to the Nacional to dance the flamenco with Lucky Luciano among the potted palms?

Was she still the wild girl hidden beneath layers of propriety and put-on sophistication? Had the layers of decorum ever really smothered the wildness of her, a wildness that had led to the death of her sister at sweet sixteen in a car accident with a drug dealer boyfriend? Had Gertrude lusted for a life of adventure with César, oh so handsome and exotic?

Eros? Life force. One and the same as death. Eros and Thanatos. Life and Death. The Greeks joined Eros with a merciless Thanatos into one figure. The Romans too. But theirs was a gentle and seductive Eros, a beautiful Ephebe holding a torch that, when tilted downwards, was their most common symbol for death.

Was César gentle at first? Certainly seductive. Oh, he could be a charmer with his movie star looks and smooth voice, its tone alone full of promise.

What's the expression? To carry a torch for someone. For an old flame, an unrequited love. Who was Gertrude's old flame? A youthful César on best behavior? The Stranger first seen on Some Enchanted Evening Across a Crowded Room? A hasty marriage. The torch soon tilted downward. Or did it? As she lay on the *de rigeur* (another favorite word of hers) hospital-cornered sheets of their bed was she César's wild girl to the last? Had the sex gotten too rough in the end?

Or had she gone to the movies? By herself? Another form of entertainment forbidden by César.

Panama Lady. Gertrude's favorite film. Mercedes was given a video copy years ago by a wannabe suitor. She needs to find it, watch it again while sorting through the residue of Gertrude's life, revisit her mother via the pixilated smugglers and murderers who stalk among the *Panama Lady* grays transferred from age-worn reels of combustible celluloid. Shadows of Gertrude's fantasy life, Hollywood style? The oil rigger McTeague, who looks to be a clone of César, falls in love with Lucille Ball. What is her character's name? Lucy plays an American nightclub hostess in Panama. (Hard to imagine Gertrude in that role, but then again, maybe not.) After a series of implausible adventures, including a close escape from a man with dishonorable intentions, Lucy ends up with McTeague.

McTeague, once teamed up with Lucy, dumps Cheema, his native woman, a woman who had killed to protect him. Oh, those fiery, wild native women! Once Cheema has furthered the plot, the movie discards her, just like McTeague did. Stereotypical racism! Cheema vanishes—like the maid Luisa vanished after César and Mercedes drove her home to her shack.

"Where's Luisa? Mommy, where's Luisa?

"She won't be coming to our house anymore."

Might the maid Luisa have been César's discarded native woman like Cheema was McTeague's? The thought had never occurred to Mercedes but now that it strikes, she finds herself crying again for Luisa over what surely must have been rape. Repeated rape. The little boy with the waggly penis who came running towards her. Or towards César? Was he César's very own "little bastard."

≈ FRESH BLOOD

She's eleven years old. It's been a year since Gertrude left César in Cuba and returned to her native Rhode Island. They've moved into an attic apartment wedged under the sloping roof of a once-elegant house in Providence that had been chopped into small units let out to widows, widowers, divorcées, and loners. Spaces "interrupted," as Gordon Matta-Clark would have said, he being the artist who sawed apart abandoned houses *somewhere between the supports and the collapse* to keep them standing. Mercedes is the only child in the house of interrupted lives. Her room affords little space to stand upright. She slides in and out of her narrow bed sideways careful not to bump her head, though often she forgets. The apartment is a far cry, as Gertrude says, from their airy, spacious home in Cuba. A far cry. Mercedes takes that to mean crying is far away, which puzzles her because she never cried when she was far away and neither did the Gertrude. César didn't cry. He yelled and screamed.

Mercedes spends summers and weekends with her grandparents on the farm while Gertrude works her first and only paid job as a secretary in a hospital in Providence. Her real job is getting another husband, a classy wealthy one.

Mercedes' life on the farm is mostly out of the house roaming the fields down to the river and climbing trees. The huge weeping beech near the house provides a canopy of concealment, and the elm at the corner of her grandmother's rose garden has thick widespread branches to sit on and lean against while she reads a book. She pretends that nobody will ever find her up in the trees, knowing they can.

Most of all, she loves the cow barn. She doesn't get there for the morning milking before the cows are let out to pasture; it's obligatory breakfast time up at the house. But she is waiting for the cows when they are brought in from pasture in the evening. They are all milked by hand. The farmer, crouched on his thick haunches behind her milking stool, his arms around her, instructs her not to yank the teats. Press finger by finger down along them like playing scales on a piano, he says.

She doesn't play the piano but quickly gets the hang of milking (pun intended). She's in charge of a specific cow. She doesn't give her a name, just loves her, loves pressing her head against the softness of the warm, full udder, loves the cow's soft groans of contentment as the discomfort of milky fullness is relieved. Milking, she's learned, releases oxytocin, pleasing and relaxing for the cow. Milking is pleasing and relaxing for her too—comforting. She loves breathing in the lingering scent of pasture, of fresh milk, fur, cow dung, and hay. The barn cats—three of them—line up at the edge of her milking stool to catch the sideways squirts of milk she aims at them. There is also a tan barn dog with a curled up tail named Gizmo who follows her up to the house, but is never allowed inside.

She grooms her cow with gusto, taking great satisfaction in getting rid of caked dirt and manure. She knows that horses are groomed, not cows. But there being no horses on the farm, she makes do with the cow. The curry brush is big and stiff-bristled but the cow seems indifferent to the harsh, energetic strokes along her back and around her big belly, merely flicking flies away from her ears now and then. Mercedes knows that cows are never very demonstrative and they have tough hides.

≈

It happened while Mercedes was grooming the cow. The farmer grabbed her from behind her back—one hairy arm around her waist, the other between her legs. He dragged her to a far, dark corner of the barn. She's quite sure she was screaming right away, but she's absolutely sure she yelled as loud as she could when he yanked her shorts and panties off. He must have loosened his grip around her waist because she was able to twist towards him. Was his fly open? His erect penis sticking out? She doesn't know. Those details are a blur or repressed or whatever you want to call it. What she does know for certain is that she was still holding the curry brush in her right hand—is certain it was her right hand. She hit him in the face with it. Hit hard hard hard hard again again again again. He must have loosened his grip on her. She ran bare-bottomed as fast as she could screaming through the barnyard gate and all the way up the long driveway to the grandparents' house.

And when she got there? Her mind is blank. Was Gertrude there? Her grandmother? Did someone wash her off? Take her to her room? Get her dressed in clean clothes? Give her a cup of hot coca? Was anything said? Questions asked?

A few days later, or maybe it was a week or two, she woke to the pawing of the dog, a Dachshund. Bravo had probably died by then and this was a replacement dog who slept on her bed sometimes. He was trying to burrow underneath the bedcovers. She lifted them. Blood. Bright red blood on her pajama bottoms and sheets. CODE RED. Once again, she screamed. Did she get out of bed? Did someone come rushing to her room?

All she remembers is being in the bathroom, the one with the black and white floor tiles near her bedroom in what had been the maids' quarters. She remembers it was Gertrude who handed her a sanitary pad and a contraption to put around her hips to fasten the ends of it. She said the blood meant Mercedes was a woman now. She didn't want to be a woman. She was eleven years old.

She spent the next few days sinking into the squishy brown ottoman chair in the back sitting room, buried under a soft brown throw, afraid to move except to waddle very slowly to the bathroom to change the bloody pads in her underpants. She kept thinking about the parrot who was shoved into a toilet and looked up at the woman with the bloody slit who sat down there. She kept hearing César's laugh.

She was afraid to eat when she was persuaded to sit down at the table. Persuaded? More like coerced, commanded.

The dog Bravo the Second was never allowed on her bed again.

≈

The farmer, who had lived in the cottage on the other side of the road beyond the cow pasture, disappeared overnight along with his wife and children. The cows disappeared too and Gizmo the dog was gone. They were his cows, not her grandparents' as Mercedes had assumed without thinking about it. Gizmo was his dog too. The farmer had merely been renting the barn, the pastures, and the cottage. The cats were not his. They hung around the house for a while but the grandparents wouldn't allow Mercedes to feed them so they too went elsewhere. That's what she wants to believe.

She was older when she found out the farmer was a known pedophile. She doesn't know who unearthed that information (not easy in the days before the internet). Who told her? How old was she? It might have been her uncle. Gertrude and the grandparents never would speak of what had happened. Her beloved uncle, out of the closet since his teens, was probably more forthcoming.

Was the farmer arrested? Or was the Incident simply ignored and he went on to molest other children? Pederasty: a sickness, a disease of the body. A virus, a virus of desire.

In the criminal justice system, sexually based offenses are considered especially heinous.

There was a time when Mercedes avidly tuned in to every episode of Law and Order SVU. Special Victims Unit. *These are their stories.* Was it to see the perpetrators brought to justice? Or to pick at an old scab.

Mercedes never went back to the barn. It remained empty, slowly rotting for many years until it too disappeared, destroyed by fire. She never asked how the fire might have been started. She only knew she was not responsible, although she was relieved when the barn was gone.

≈ THE WHITE BLOUSE

Mercedes was thirteen when Gertrude moved to Connecticut to the home of her new husband, George-the-Lawyer. Living her early teens amid the uptight good manners of the big brick mansion and its manicured surround, where arguments took the form of tiny barbs tipped with poisonous chuckles, Mercedes came to see César as a tempestuous soul whose Latino nature had been frustrated and misunderstood. César's monstrosity became poetic, a thrilling life force. *Evil is more powerful in the human psyche* (William James). César was Mercedes's wild savage, his desires primitive, untamed, raw. He was her Object of Desire, her Exotic Territory, her Transgressive Other, academic phrases later familiar to her, phrases that drain romantic longing and bodily urges of their sticky, moist, pulsing teenage force.

No body touched another body in Connecticut. Perfunctory social embraces involved both parties leaning forward at an angle, hands barely grazing shoulders, cheeks a half-inch apart. The men never told off-color jokes during the cocktail hour; they pontificated about the stock market and ranted over excessive taxes and liberal politics. Instead of whisky, they sipped decorous martinis with green olives.

When Mercedes was commandeered to pass the cheese and crackers, guests figured she was a maid. Then, when introduced as Gertrude's daughter, they assumed she was adopted from Guatemala, the most popular country for procuring babies at the time. Neither mother or daughter wanted to correct the misunderstanding.

As for Gertrude, tight-lipped smile firmly in place, she had shriveled into a woman without passion, without even routine thump, thump sex, a privation Mercedes suspected long before Gertrude confessed, after more than a few cocktails, that when she married George, he was already "not the man he used to be." George's belting out *Yes! We have no bananas*, his favorite song from college days, took on new meaning after that revelation. If César hadn't entirely snuffed the life out of Gertrude, George finished the job.

In old age George had to urinate with unpredictable frequency. A clear glass container was slotted in a holder of his walker for emergencies. He didn't bother to put the sloshy jar in a bag; it stayed in full view next to him, even during meals. Closest he ever came to sexual abuse. But that was much later when Gertrude was already a bit demented.

During those teen years in Connecticut, Mercedes had not forgotten César's cocktail hour show times, night visits, Fuzo's execution, hidden liquor bottles, and temper tantrums. But memories, like people, acquire different accents when moved to new territory. Mercedes took to carrying a yellowing, dog-eared photo of her father taken before she was born slid into a plastic slot in her wallet facing a headshot of James Dean. Jimmy's pained moodiness bled over to César's gorgeous profile as both men gazed into a mysterious distance.

She had just turned sixteen when Aunt Lola called to say that César was coming to visit her and he wanted to see his daughter. He'd moved from Cuba to San Antonio immediately after Gertrude had left him and married a Mexican, Dolores, who would accompany him.

Mercedes didn't like Dolores, sight unseen. Her name alone, *dolor*, meaning "pain" in Spanish, was already a put off. The cousins, Aunt Lola's boys, had whispered that Dolores had been married to a defrocked priest—defrocked because he couldn't keep his hands off her. And Aunt Lola had told her that Dolores was one of Mexico's earliest psychotherapists. Dolores! What a name for a shrink! Mercedes got Christmas cards from her signed with César's name without her bothering to fake his handwriting. The cards were Mercedes's only contact with her father during the six years since she'd left Cuba. That is, aside from Aunt Lola's occasional updates and the court-mandated checks he sent Gertrude for their daughter's expenses.

César's impending proximity set Mercedes into a panic.

"Why would he want to see me?" she asked. "You know he never writes. He doesn't even sign the Christmas cards from Dolores."

"Well he *will* want to see you," Aunt Lola rebutted, her gentle voice resolute.

Mercedes started obsessing over what to wear. She bought a lacy bra a size too big and experimented with stuffing it with toilet paper and wads of cotton. She already had a wide red cinch belt she hoped made her square body look curvy. Gertrude forbade her to wear it, but she planned to tuck it into her big purse and stretch it around her waist as soon as she left the house.

Makes you look cheap, was Gertrude's opinion.

The morning of the visit she jolted awake from a dream, heartbeat jagged: she had to pack a suitcase with small open containers of clear liquid—little shot glasses. Whatever it was, it was splattering all over. She knew these were dreams spilling out, but she told herself that dreams aren't liquid.

Aunt Lola came to pick her up. At the last minute Mercedes ditched the cinch belt, but not the stuffed bra, her burgeoning tissue breasts camouflaged with a loose jacket.

She was grateful for the half hour drive alone with her aunt who wanted to know about school, friends, books, but did not mention Gertrude or George. As they were nearing the house, Aunt Lola told her that César had had an accident that had damaged one hand and that he would be wearing a glove over it. Mercedes was to pretend not to notice and not ask any questions.

"Why? What was the accident?"

"Never mind. I've promised not to talk about it."

The minute Mercedes walked through the door she could tell he'd been drinking though his voice was smooth as ever. His clothes too. Crisply pressed gray slacks, white shirt, and a smooth brown sweater that had to be cashmere. The glove that Mercedes did her best not to look at was a matching soft brown leather. Still the classy dresser.

"You've grown," he said.

"I'm sixteen."

"I guess that's right." He planted a quick nervous kiss on her cheek. A waft of minty whiskey breath sent a cold shudder down to the pit of Mercedes' belly.

From across the room Dolores whooped, "Mercedes, *carina*! I am Dolores!" The next moment she'd flung her buxom, gardenia-scented body into the breach and wrapped Mercedes in a hug so fierce it disrupted the cotton and toilet paper stuffed into her new bra. Loud liposuction kisses on both cheeks followed.

"*Que bonita*! César, what a lovely daughter you have!"

Lovely? Ha! Mercedes thought. I'm not *bonita*, not even close. An array of metal tortured her errant teeth towards even rows. Thick round glasses magnified her blue eyes into an even greater unworldliness, a look bolstered by a scattering of partially squeezed pimples that made her face resemble the surface of a distant planet. All framed by two hanks of hair styled by Monsieur André at Gertrude's insistence. Mercedes was subjected daily to her mother's dismayed mantra: Beauty comes from within, dear.

The three cousins, gangly ginger-haired boys in their teens who bore an uncanny resemblance to their grandpapa O'Brian, were standing by numbly.

"Hi," Mercedes said, nodding in their direction.

"Hi," they nodded back.

Mercedes avoided the sofa, skittering over to a chair where she could be sure of not being next to either César or Dolores. From there, she got a good look at César, who had seated himself at the far side of the room. He'd put on a lot of weight. In six years he'd become an old man, a fat old man, nothing like the handsome navy officer in the photo taken before Mercedes was born. His face was very red, crisscrossed with jagged veins that rushed towards his nose. His watery eyes avoided his daughter. Mercedes immediately regretted having bought the lacy bra. She thanked her lucky stars at least she hadn't worn the cinch belt.

Dolores's blaring voice was resounding off every surface and crevice of the room. Not even the carpets and upholstery were spared. Mercedes shifted automatically into a state of numbness, a talent she'd been perfecting since childhood. She still heard the voice, but as if it were far away and speaking a language unknown to her, a distant avalanche of gushing sounds without connotations. She was jerked out of her otherworldly state when Dolores, still jabbering, thrust a big box onto her lap. It was wrapped in pink and gold striped paper, bound by a wide pink ribbon with a bow that had lots of loops.

Well, open it! Dolores shouted. A present. For you, from your father and me. She kept on as if Mercedes were mentally challenged or otherwise deranged. Deaf too. "You can open it, you know. It is for you. Your very own present from me and your father."

Let me get you some scissors, Aunt Lola interrupted.

No! You don't need scissors. Just pull, like so. Dolores gave the pink ribbon a yank.

Thank you, Mercedes sighed, not to Dolores, but to Aunt Lola, who was approaching, scissors in hand. It was a relief to have her nearby—and armed.

The ribbon stripped away, tossed aside by Dolores, Mercedes had no choice but to remove the striped paper and open the box, a cardboard box coated shiny white. Inside, nestled amid reams of pink tissue paper, was a white blouse. It was a cross between a frilly garment for a baby and one for a hooker whose appeal depended on girlishness. Its prim Peter Pan collar and short puffed sleeves were suitable for a child, but not the transparent chiffon fabric. It was like the dresses César would buy for her to wear at cocktail hour.

"Try it on! Try it on!" Dolores was urging.

"Later, when I get home."

"No, now Mercedes! We want to see how pretty you will look."

Mercedes looked over at Aunt Lola.

"Let's go up to my bedroom," she said.

In the sanctuary of her bedroom, Aunt Lola let out a sigh and gently hugged her niece close. "Just put it on and get back out there. She shrugged. Diplomacy. It's been enough of a struggle to get your father to pay your expenses, even with a lawyer for a husband."

Mercedes had never told Aunt Lola about the cocktail hour show times in Havana, but it didn't take much to see how upset she was. Even Dolores might have noticed.

"We've got to pick our battles," Aunt Lola said. "I'll take you home right after. Forget about staying for lunch."

She eased Mercedes out of her shirt as if she were a burn victim whose clothes had to be removed ever so tenderly. Wordlessly, she threw away the cotton and toilet paper slopping out of the bra. Devoid of stuffing, it hung limp and puckered.

"Better take it off," she said, and went to get a cotton chemise from her bureau. "This might be a little big, but you have to put something on under this see-through thing."

Mercedes liked the way she said "thing," the blouse an object that didn't deserve a name.

Back in the living room Dolores was still gabbing away. In fact, Mercedes had heard her the entire time she'd been upstairs in the bedroom. How could you be a shrink and never stop talking?

Mercedes must have zoned out again during her brief catwalk because the next thing she remembers is being in the car with Aunt Lola on her way back to Gertrude and George's house.

"Bad idea," Aunt Lola said. "I'm sorry."

"It's OK. I'll survive."

Aunt Lola enveloped Mercedes in comforting silence for the rest of the drive. Mercedes might have fallen asleep, but towards the end she roused herself to ask about César's gloved hand.

"I'll never see him again, so you can tell me."

"I promised Joe I wouldn't. He's the only one who knew what happened, and that's because your father asked Joe to meet him at the military hospital in San Antonio."

"I won't tell Uncle Joe you told."

"I guess it doesn't matter anymore. Your father's hand was cut off. What's under the glove is a prosthetic."

"Why? What happened?"

"The cook did it. The cook Inmaculada you were always telling me about. She did it after your mother left Cuba and she found out that you weren't coming back to Havana."

Inmaculada! Even when she knew she'd never see me again, she protected me. Mercedes smiled, calling to mind the big swoop of Inmaculada's cleaver as she told the story of Abraham and Isaac. Had she put César's hand on the block as she did the chickens' necks before slicing their heads off clean? It was César's right hand she severed, his pistol hand, the hand he used to shoot Fuzo. His playtime hand.

What happened to her? Mercedes asked.

She disappeared and the police could never find her.

Of course the police couldn't find her. Mercedes remembers Inmaculada's tales of her policemen brothers and cousins and her uncle strongmen who would do whatever it took to protect and avenge one of their own. Like Inmaculada herself. Only then did Mercedes understand why César never set foot in Inmaculada's kitchen. And why he never dared fire her.

The Christmas cards signed by Dolores continued to appear with dogged regularity. Mercedes stopped opening them once she realized there was never going to be a check enclosed.

≈ SECRETS

Mercedes' cousin Henry, one of Lola's sons, insisted she attend her father's funeral at Annapolis where a slot on a high gray wall of similar slots gaped open to receive his ashes. Henry is the only person she knows who liked César, "warts and all," he said.

Several rows of gray folding chairs are set up under a tent in front of a pulpit. Mercedes and Henry are the only ones there. They sit in the front row.

Aunt Lola is significantly absent. I hated my brother all my life, she told Mercedes when they met for tea a day or so before the funeral. It was then she revealed that César had tried to rape her when she was nine years old. He was fifteen. Her mother heard her screams. Rushing into her daughter's bedroom, she pulled her son, pants down around his knees, off her little girl's body prone on the floor. The incident was never mentioned by a living soul. Aunt Lola was eighty when she told Mercedes. She never told her children. Certainly not Henry.

Rape. *Violación.*

Strange fruit dangle from trees in Arizona: panties and bras, limp trophies hung by coyotes who gang raped the little girls and women they smuggled into the US. Rape trees. It was Carina, a homeless woman at Passages where Mercedes volunteered to help with housing applications, who told her about the trees at the border. Carina was ten when she was raped by the smuggler her mother had paid.

Mesquite trees, skimpy and tenacious, flourishing in the inhospitable terrain of Arizona, flaunt pink, yellow, red, blue, and white undies draped on the branches. Blood on the leaves and blood at the roots. Blood on the ground—rape blood, red fading to pink as it seeps into the pale desert sand. Rape trees. Pink panties. Women and girls raped not only by smugglers, but by US border patrol too. Rape. *Violación.* Everywhere in whatever language you call it.

After a brief service followed by a twelve-gun salute Henry and Mercedes leave. She gives him the folded American flag that was handed to her. She puts the empty bullet casings in her purse to arrange on a shelf at home, a memorial of sorts. She does not betray Aunt Lola's secret.

≈ SHIPS AHOY

Swell of dizziness, rush of heat, armpits and crotch sticky wet, heartbeat breaking jagged. Deep breath, Mercedes tells herself as she leans forward to open a large box labeled CÉSAR, the last remaining item in the trunk. He's dead, she tells herself, and looks up at the row of twelve bullet casings on her shelf.

César. There must have been a shred of something besides libido and raging dominance in him. He was her father, for Christ's sake, her father! If she goes on hating him, she'll end up just like him. *Whoever fights monsters should see to it that in the process he doesn't become a monster* (Nietzsche). Open the box!

She lifts out a hefty book. The Naval Academy yearbook: *Ships Ahoy* (1935). Oh yes, she remembers it well. César would bring it out to show to company, carefully turning the pages as if it were a rare sacred text. She was forbidden to touch it, not even to lay a tiny finger on the heavy black cover, never mind the numerous gold-tinted, full-page illustrations of John Paul Jones, the "Father of the American Navy." César's hero. Now she takes vengeful pleasure in swiping her hand over the decorative pictures. Desecration of the sacred patriarchal text.

Turning to César's bio page, she realizes with a start that there's not an accent over the "e." He's Cesar. Typo? She checks his name in the index, in the entries for committees and sports teams. Not an accent anywhere. All traces of *De Allá*, From Over There, whitewashed away. His nickname? Francis. Not a tough guy moniker—Wild Man, Brutus, Whack, Thug—tags given to many other cadets. Nor a playful one—Jinks, Punchy, Angel Face, Foo-Foo. Oh no. Francis, César's middle name, is his nickname. Who has a middle name as a nickname, especially if it happens to be Francis?

Mercedes has long realized ethnic shame could account, in part, for César's battles against everyone and everything. Threat too in being identified as *De Allá*. Even if you're a legal US citizen, you're still alien. Legal aliens. Back when César was at Annapolis two million people were deported to Mexico, more than half born in the US. César was born in Mexico, already six years old when the family immigrated to New Jersey. Today they all would have been stuffed into overcrowded camps rife with disease at the border. César along with Aunt Lola and Uncle Joe might have been separated from Grandpapa and Grandmama. César, could have been that crying little boy wearing an oversized red t-shirt clinging to his mother's thigh. Then lost. Dead perhaps. All dead, children and parents. The horror.

But maybe, with an Irish head of household they would have been given special treatment. Might the name O'Brian have counted for something if a patrol guard happened to be Irish?

She turns back to the yearbook. The blurb below Francis's class photograph notes that he was always seen at the hops with one of "the fairest of the fair" on his arm. Prototypes of Gertrude. Yes, he would have had to marry a blonde. Was he hoping for blond descendants? A tall, strapping blond boy? Certainly not a stocky, dark-skinned daughter!

Folded into the yearbook are three documents. There's a certificate of honorable discharge dated 1937, a mere two years after his graduation from the naval academy, and an official recall back to service from 1939, a few weeks before Mercedes was born. Germany had invaded Poland and the war had begun in earnest. A foreign invasion accounts for her father's absence when she was little. And for so many children whose fathers would never come home again. The military commandeered every available man, even criminals doing jail time. Alcoholics? Why not. Sex offenders? No problem. John Paul Jones, daddy of the navy, who fled Russia after he did something he shouldn't have done to a ten-year-old butter seller named Katherine, was the first shining example.

A second honorable discharge for poor eyesight is dated 1942. The US Navy had defeated the Japanese. César had perfect vision.

So that was it too. Double disgrace. Shame, dishonor, humiliation, ignominy. Honorable this and honorable that, blah, blah, blah. César knew he had 20/20 eyesight. A wetback with perfect vision.

Wetback. Mercedes is stopped short by the insult coming to mind. How often might César have heard it? Directed at him. But not in the navy, where he'd erased all traces of an accent in speech and name. Then kicked out. Twice! Left with no measure of his preeminence other than a yearbook and bogus honorable discharges.

An erased accent mark, Tres Flores hair pomade always with him to smooth away the kinks, thoroughbred attack Dobermans to protect him. Of course he had to kill Fuzo, a mutt like himself.

Hatred roiling his innards to erupt at the slightest deviation of a carpet fringe. No carpets in a submarine. No room for irregularities. Explains a lot. A life full of sound and fury, signifying nothing. Zilch. Diddly-squat. But that's no excuse. Pity him, maybe. Pity his shame, his fears, his weakness and insecurity, but pity, an arrogant emotion at that, doesn't let him off the hook.

Explanations and understandings do not equal forgiveness.

Forgive? Pardon, absolve, exculpate, let it go. Antonyms? Hold on, keep it tight. Be merciless. Without mercy.

Mercy, Lord have mercy, Grandmama would murmur, her stout figure swathed in black pacing the New Jersey living room, hands fingering the strands of her pearly gray rosary. She'd worn black as long as Mercedes can remember, long before Grandpapa died. For whom? *Dios, ten piedad. Piedad.* Pity. Who was she thinking of? César, her firstborn? Pity. She didn't ask for forgiveness. Didn't say, *Dios perdonalo.* God forgive him. No. *Piedad*, she whispered. Pity.

Was pity the only way Grandmama could love her oldest son? Is pity the only way Mercedes can feel anything close to love for her father? Could pity give her an escape hatch, a way to rid herself of the hatred she feels for him. Could pity shove hatred out like a bag of garbage down a chute? Even when she had a teenage crush on him, she'd despised him. Cocktail hour, parrot drowning in a toilet, Fuzo. All that was there too.

She's been bound to César by hatred, bound more tightly than if she'd loved a kind, gentle father. Always the little girl hiding in her room at cocktail hour wearing the fancy dress her papa bought, dreading and, yes, hoping he would come for her. César, her father César, has been her ongoing passion. What will be left without the hatred? Pity. *Piedad.* Passion's refuse.

Seated in front of the empty trunk, she catches sight of a mottled photograph she'd slipped into it years ago. She'd rescued it from a stack of papers in her friend Katia's flooded basement.

"Who's in the picture?" Mercedes had asked.

"The little girl? That's me. I know that's my father in the background even if you can't really see him."

"Mind if I keep it?"

"Sure. Although you can't make out much in it." Katia's tone was politely puzzled. "I have other family photos, if you want."

"Thanks, but this one will do."

Blotched and smeared to abstraction, the two figures a ghostly blue, the girl in the foreground has resisted the total obliteration by water. Two pinpoints of eyes set in a smiling chubby face stare out from under thick blue-black bangs. Of the washed away shape of the father looming behind the child only an arm resting on the little girl's shoulder is visible. Father and daughter are as if underwater, drifting in a tangle of seaweeds. The father, annihilated by water, reaches for the child, for the sea creature she has become.

The one picture Mercedes has of her with her father and it's not of them.

≈ FAMILY CREST

On the floor next to the trunk is a framed reproduction of the O'Brian family crest that she's put aside. The coat of arms. It is fixed in her mind even more solidly than *Ships Ahoy*. César had not one but three identical pictures of it, all displayed under glass and framed in expensive mahogany (as he would note).

Lámh láidir in Uachtar reads its motto.

The ghost of César fills the room. Low LAW-jir un OO-ukh-tur, he proclaims in his melodic voice, rhyming "low" with "cow." Bhí an lámh in uachtar agam air, he continues with a sardonic chuckle.

"I got the upper hand on him," he translates.

The only Gaelic phrase César knew, but he made it go a long way. He must have known the history of the disembodied arm on the crest, but he never told Mercedes the story of the warrior king whose arm it was. It was Grandpapa O'Brian, a true Irish seanchaí, who told Mercedes their ancestral stories on visits to New Jersey. She was his favorite grandchild, the only girl and she looked like his beloved wife, Meche.

"Come sit by me and I'll tell you a story," he'd say. Cuddled next to him, she'd listen, watching his scraggly white beard waggle with his words.

It was from him that she learned the legend of King Nuada.

"Once upon a time there was a king named Nuada. That's his arm holding a sword that you see here on the crest. Nuada in Old Gaelic means 'cloud maker' and that's why King Nuada's arm is coming out of a cloud."

"Did he really make clouds? Grandmama says God makes clouds from where he is up in the sky."

"Cloud Maker is just what he was called, probably because people who didn't believe in God were mistaken and thought it was King Nuada who made the clouds. That was a very long time ago."

"Do you believe in God, Grandpapa?"

"Yes, I do. Let's get on with the story."

"Inmaculada believes in God."

"Nuada," continued Grandpapa O'Brian, "was king of the Tuatha Dé people."

"Who were the Tuatha Dé?"

"They were people who weren't yet Irish. Mercedes, if you keep asking questions, we'll never finish the story."

"I'm sorry. I won't ask any more questions."

"After seven years of being king, Nuada decided he and the Tuatha Dé should live in Ireland."

Mercedes wanted to ask why after seven years and why Ireland, but she kept quiet.

"So," Grandpapa would continue, "Nuada and the Tuatha Dé got in touch with the Fir Bolg." He paused seeing the questioning look on Mercedes's face. "The Fir Bolg were the folk who lived in Oirlan' way back then."

Even though Grandpapa O'Brian's family had left Ireland for Mexico when he was a young boy and he spoke English with more of a Mexican accent than a brogue, when he told old Irish tales he would begin ta spake a few words 'ere an' dare like a true Oirishman. But in pronouncing "Nuada" it sounded like the Spanish word "nada," meaning nothing, especially when he said it fast. King Nada. King Nothing. That's how Mercedes remembered the name for years thereafter.

"Nuada asked the Fir Bolg for alf of Oilan for the Tuatha Dé. No way, said the Fir Bolg king." (Grandpapa would lapse into Americanisms as easily as he would slip into brogue.)

Grandpapa O'Brian went on to tell how the Tuatha Dé and the Fir Bolg made ready for war, how both sides allowed their soldiers and weapons to be inspected by the opposing army so the battle would be truly fair.

"That was very nice," Mercedes said.

"Wars were different back then," he commented.

"During this great battle," Grandpapa went on, "King Nuada lost an arm in combat with the Fir Bolg champion Sreng. Fifty soldiers carried Nuada from the field."

"Fifty? That's a lot of soldiers."

"They had to defend him from getting hurt even more."

"Oh."

Grandpapa started to push himself up from the sofa. "Time for lunch."

"Wait! Then what happened?"

A robust aroma of *aroz con pollo* wafted into the living room from the kitchen, prompting Grandpapa O'Brian to summarize the story post haste without a trace of an Irish accent.

"The Tuatha Dé won the battle, but the defeated King Sreng later challenged King Nuada to one-on-one combat. Nuada accepted, but only if King Sreng fought with one arm tied up."

"Because King Nuada had only one arm?"

"Right."

"King Sreng refused to fight with only one arm, but it didn't matter because he'd already been defeated. King Nuada and the Tuatha Dé decided to offer King Sreng one quarter of Ireland for his people."

"Even after he lost the battle?"

"Yep. He chose the province of Connacht."

"Is that where we come from?"

"Heck no, Mercedes. We are descended from King Nuada. That's why we have the family crest."

By this point in the tale, Grandpapa O'Brian was already in the dining room and easing himself into his chair at the head of the table. Grandmama hadn't yet scuttled into the room to serve his meal, so he continued his story.

"Because he lost his arm, Nuada couldn't be king anymore. The Tuatha Dé tradition was that their king had to be physically perfect."

"That's not fair."

"It ended up OK. Nuada got a new arm and became king again and ruled for twenty more years."

Mercedes will keep the picture of the family crest but not the heavy frame César had imposed around it. She turns it over to its papered reverse, sliding her fingernail along the edges to release King Nuada from César's dark enclosure.

King Nuada got a new arm. Wars were nicer back then. Maybe there can be civility and compassion again. She feels lighter, as if she could levitate from the carpeted floor, flutter through the windows of her apartment into the park across the street, fresh blood pulsing in her veins. *Preciosa mariposa.*

≈ SOONER OR LATER

Police killings. Racism erupts for everyone to see. Protests grow urgent, angry, violent. Curfews imposed starting at 8:00 p.m. Police cars wail, not only ambulances carrying those stricken with the Virus. Helicopters circle over the park across the street night and day. Mercedes ventures out less and less. Stress. Anxiety. Will this ever end?

She is getting even more ditzy. More confused. More forgetful. Everything takes concentration. The effort not to screw up is exhausting. Vigilant. Constantly vigilant. Lists and post-its proliferate—stuck to the computer, the kitchen cabinets, and the mirror in the bathroom, where they drift steamily down into the sink—petals of dying flowers. She does a lot these days to prove, mostly to herself in quarantine, that she's capable.

She's nibbling at her fingernails, a habit she'd broken years ago, along with cigarettes. Onychophagia. From the Greek. She could never picture Achilles or Odysseus biting their nails to the quick, but maybe Penelope.

What will become of her? To become. Becoming. A process. She or he is becoming an actor, a writer, a hematologist, a botanist, a Somebody that she or he previously was not. We're always becoming something. Becoming excited, tired, fearful … Becoming demented?

Unbecoming. That's another story. Think about it later.

Start a Falling Into Dementia journal? Separate file. Would that make her even more paranoid? No, paranoid isn't the word she's searching for. The word she wants is the one for excessive worry about one's health. Typical of her father. Biological father that is. BIO LOGICAL. Bio for biology, bio for biography. Logical? Nothing was logical with her biological father. He was paranoid as well as … What's that word? Won't come. Shit. He was always thinking he was sick. Then he was and boy oh boy did we all hear about it. How can you leave the bedside of a dying man to go visit your aunt, he'd said. This after she'd been with him all morning and was returning that afternoon. Hypochondriac! Found the word. Maybe she's also a hypochondriac.

Words. Their growing elusiveness is the most worrisome development. Development? No, regression. Not regression. Not yet. For now, words are merely sluggish, slow to surface at times, hiding themselves. Not only proper names—less used, always the first to go—but all sorts of words, familiar words that used to come to mind without bidding. Beloved arcane words too were there when she needed them and rippling along even when she didn't.

She's developed coping strategies. Substitutions. Associations. The other day it was for "adrenaline." The word would come back with effort, then disappear. She'd find it again tucked in some remote corner of the hippocampus and write it down. But without the note, she couldn't bring it up again. She tried various mnemonic devices with little success until she came up with "I dread linen." That helps—for now. But she can't remember why it was important to remember the word "adrenaline." What had she been thinking about? Never mind.

Names are even more difficult to coax out of hiding. Stubborn. She struggled for the name of an actor whose face, admittedly unforgettable, was crystal clear. "Wallet shorn" was her solution. Wally Shawn!

Why is it easier to remember something by remembering something else? You'd think it would take more effort to keep two things in mind. Maybe because "I dread linen" is an emotion and "wallet shorn" is an object, a torn one at that. Fear and mutilation. What does that say about her! About the times she's living. Fear and mutilation. Protests. Counter-protests.

For a good chunk of her adult life, Mercedes's greatest fear has been that, like her mother, her entire self, the who of her—an already troubled, precarious identity—will be obliterated while her body still lives and breathes. She hopes her father's genetics will predominate. No dementia on that side of the sporogenus border. Hypochondria and rampant paranoia and rage, but not dementia.

Has she now become like her mother was when her mind began to go AWOL? But, if so, there's a difference. A big difference. Mercedes is not in denial. Not like her mother who threw pencils and a stapler at her doctor when told she had the beginnings of dementia. She would have hurled his big mahogany desk if she could have before she stomped out of the room. Nonsense! Total nonsense, she yelled, her words unwittingly defining her condition. She could still walk and talk then.

Mercedes, on the other hand, brought up her concerns with Nathan, whose job it was to pay unconditional attention to her for forty-five minutes once a week. He saw no signs of dementia. Trauma, he said. A lingering PTSD can cause forgetfulness. You had a rough time as a kid.

PTSD. Maybe. Mercedes' memory has always been unreliable. In high school she'd select a visual anchor for each event studied in history class. Byzantine big-eyed Emperor Justinian. Clunky, jagged-edged Rosetta stone: two languages, three scripts. Queen Hatshepsut wearing the false beard of a pharaoh. *Washington Crossing the Delaware* painted by an artist whose name she's forgotten along with the reason for the crossing. She's always been able to conjure up the objects, it's the facts, the very reason she memorized the objects, that elude her. Facts are invisible.

Maybe what's happening now isn't dementia, just normal aging, a few wrinkles in the brain like on her upper arms. That's what everyone tells her. Not the wrinkly, saggy arms part—just a normal aging brain, they say. (It was the dermatologist who told her the wrinkly arms were normal. You're thin-skinned, he'd said.)

Not totally convinced, she went to a graying neurologist who looked like the type to play golf on weekends. (That was in the days when doctors' offices were still open!) He had her count from one hundred back to one in multiples of seven and repeat a string of unrelated words after a break of unrelated conversation. "You're fine. Your problem is you don't always concentrate. No need for tests," he concluded.

A kindly second doctor, Dr. Kelly, ordered an MRI, "Just to put your mind at ease."

Mild volume loss and microvascular ischemic disease. No acute infarct, according to the test results.

Ischemic disease? Infarct? Whatever that is, at least it's not acute. But what about the ischemic disease?

Dr. Kelly explained that microvascular ischemic disease is the rupturing or clotting of tiny blood vessels in small areas in the brain. "Very few in your case. Not uncommon for your age," he added.

"And infarct?"

"The death of a little bit of living tissue, but nothing to worry about at this point."

"At this point! But what about ..."

"Well, microvascular changes can build up over time and microvascular disease is the second leading cause of dementia after Alzheimer's, but it is not always progressive. That said, given the dementia on your mother's side and your moments of confusion and memory loss, I suggest another checkup in a couple of years. "

Microvascular ischemic disease. Three authoritive, defining words that further upended her sense of self, of who she is and who she may become.

Quarantine because of the pandemic came as a relief. Admit it. Out in the world she'd become anxious going to unfamiliar places. Walking crowded streets had become hazardous, confusing. Too much coming at her from all directions. Never was a problem, even before cell phones and even when she travelled alone in countries where a language she didn't know was spoken. Look at a map. No problem. That's what everyone says even when there is a problem.

A booming blast followed by a racket of metal clanging and pinging startles Mercedes out of her thoughts. She rushes to the window, opens it a crack, cautiously peers out. Whoosh of rushing water.

The torrent capsizes a metal trash can and swirls its garbage along the road: plastic bags of dog poop, Starbucks paper cups, food-splattered Styrofoam containers, used napkins, newspapers, half masticated hotdogs and bagels, whorls of brightly colored leaflets … A crowd is gathering on the steps leading up to the park. Sirens wail the arrival of fire engines.

A water main has burst, erupted out from under the street, tearing through asphalt as if it were cardboard. She's seen this on TV, but never right in front of her. And never in the midst of a world-wide pandemic and protests and shootings. The explosion is flooding her street.

Manhattan's old pipes can't hold the force of water forever. Sooner or later everything has to give way. Cerebral arteries give way. Words get lost in streams of confusion, arthritic knees buckle, skin sags, thousands die of a new Virus, the planet heats up to extinction.

≈

When she was seven Mercedes almost drowned. Someone, undoubtedly another child, pushed her into the deep end of a pool. She remembers thrashing to the surface again and again then going limp, sinking to the bright blue concrete bottom. Children squiggled in the water above as she drifted down. This too she remembers. But it is the sense of detachment and peace as she surrendered to the water that she returns to again and again. The moment before oblivion.

Then she was belly-flat on the hard, rough tiles at the edge of the pool. Someone was pumping her back. Push. Push. Push. Water spewed from her mouth. Vomit too. A rescue persistent and brutal she'd rather forget. The letting go that came before, the giving of herself to the water, is the memory she holds dear.

Unlike many people who have almost drowned, Mercedes grew to love being in water. Even the chilly waters of New England beaches, waters that had left her huddled on the shore as a child, blue-lipped and shivering. But she gloried most in the warmer waters of lakes and ponds and tropical oceans. And, despite the harsh chlorine, she was glad for indoor pools where she could swim within a clearly demarcated lane and see her shadow glide between the black lines that indicated her place, her trajectory.

Whatever the body of water, as she swooped beneath it to surface into the ecstatic rhythms of a long lazy crawl she entered another dimension, one liberated from the world of hard, unyielding surfaces. The fleshiness of her dissolved to become one with water. Suffering and rage transmuted into grace and beauty. She swam sidestroke, breaststroke, backstroke, even butterfly, her body undulating like an eel. Earplugs and cap and the swish of water reduced the outside sounds of chatter and flapping flipflops to a soft, indistinguishable murmur as her mind quieted along with the quieting of all the beyond water.

≈

Looking out at the water flooding her street, a thought strikes—a plan. A reassuring plan. Should memories and words progressively fade into oblivion, she'll slide down into deep waters. Slide down to the ocean's depths to join the remains of lost ships and vanished treasures. Yes. And she will load her pockets with stones of all shades and shapes and sizes. Beautiful stones she will select one by one.

She imagines Virginia Woolf carefully selected the stones to weigh down her pockets for her final walk into the river Ouse. She knows Hart Crane folded his coat neatly over the railing of the boat before he leaped to his death in the Caribbean. *Syllables want breath,* he'd written. Did he hold his breath as he plunged into the water?

She will be like the Mother of Waters in one of Inmaculada's favorite tales. She pictures Inmaculada wiggling and squirming her big black body as she acts out the story of this serpent so enormous she could swallow a man whole. "But only bad men and never little children," Inmaculada assures Mercedes. "She lives in rivers and when it is her time to die she slithers all the way to the ocean. That's her real home. She knows when the time has come to return to the place where she was born."

Preciosa mariposa, Mercedes whispers. She was a precious butterfly back then. But never again after Cuba.

She's read that the one thing that a butterfly cannot do is grow. Growth is the specialty of the wormy caterpillar. A new perspective on death to keep in mind.

The new butterfly self takes getting used to, requires preparation. It's not just one, two, three, and fly away. Oh no. Newly emerged from its chrysalis, the butterfly has to inflate its wings with blood, new blood, the blood of the creature it has become. And the wings have to dry, an hour or even three, a big chunk of time for a butterfly. Maybe years in human time. During this blooding up and drying off, the butterfly's only protection from predators is its elaborate camouflage. *A play of intricate enchantment and deception*, is how Nabokov put it. In addition to his fame as a writer, he was a renowned butterfly genitalist, the uniqueness of butterfly genitalia being one of the most important elements in their taxonomic identification.

Yet a butterfly is merely a transformed caterpillar, an old caterpillar, a senior citizen fluttering its colorful last, the exuberant, brief dying of a crawling slug. She's reminded again of Anatole Broyard who became a butterfly as he was dying, free to let out his craziness in all its garish colors.

She will emerge from her cocoon, once again a butterfly fluttering its last bit of life.

It's not death people fear. What they fear is the incompleteness of their lives. She will die full-circle back to where it all began.

> *Drowning is not so pitiful*
> *As the attempt to rise...*   Emily Dickinson

≈ CLUTTER BEGONE

The business of putting her home and affairs in order takes on more urgency every day. What to throw away? Give away? To whom? To charities? Which ones? Decisions that never came easy. Night after night she dreams of miscellaneous stuff scattered helter skelter throughout her home. She's dashing from room to room trying to make order, but things keep accumulating: shirts, sweaters, socks, dishes, pots, glasses, books, notepads. Unidentified objects tumble off shelves, spill out of drawers and closets.

The bulk of her belongings are from thrift shops—sofas, chairs, tables, bookshelves, dishes, and clothes too. They've gathered themselves in her home, floated in and come to rest where they belong. Belong. Her belongings.

She's never gone along with Sartre's claim that the self doesn't distinguish between what is "me" and what is "mine," but maybe he had a point. Her belongings. She belongs to them as much as they belong to her.

An installation by an artist—damn, what was his name?—comes to her mind. He placed all his personal belongings on display and invited viewers to take whatever they wanted. Mercedes was drawn back to the gallery again and again, but couldn't bring herself to carry away a single item. When she visited the final day nothing was left. It had been like witnessing an agonizingly slow suicide. *The loss of possessions is a partial conversion of oneself to nothingness* (William James).

It's not just *what* Mercedes lives with, it's *who* she lives with. People and experiences belong to her belongings. Every single object has its personal history, its own personality. Possessions are haunted by wisps of recollections. The hand puppet nestled into her life on a bookshelf, its sagging cloth body and little wood feet dangling down in front of Nabokov's *Speak Memory* reminds her of Emily and their yoga trip to Costa Rica. Sharp-eyed Emily was the one who spied the puppets in a dim back corner of a gas station convenience store. The little windup toys are from Tim's extensive collection that he brought one at a time when he'd visit from Maine. She smiles remembering how Tim could get wound up too. A slender yellow vase, a gift from Cheryl, brings her Botticelli face and cascade of copper hair to mind. How often will she think of Bruna without her little pebble sprouting a jingle bell that tinkles when she brushes by? Bruna, artist of the unexpected: a canoe traverses a river—suspended in the air.

Keepsakes: keep for the sake [of]. *The precious keepsakes, into which is wrought the giver's loving though*t. (Longfellow) Loving thoughts will be stripped from her keepsakes. New sentiments will clothe them as they pass on to other people, people she will never know.

No close friends, no immediate family, only objects. Things have become her friends and family. She's never thought of it that way. Frigging dismal. All things grasped too tightly reduce life to property, reduce memories to property. What happened to the fleshiness of her life?

A widow destroyed all photographs of her husband. Her memories of him—his voice, his scent, his changing expressions, his walk, the tilt of his head, his million little gestures—were all being replaced by the immobility of the photographs she'd propped around her home. She tore every last one to shreds, threw the scraps away to recover what had been the livingness of him. Iconoclasm makes perfect sense. The essence of knowing and believing, the holiness of it, gets lost, or at best marginalized by representation. It's for the best there were no pictures of the maids in the *geniza*.

Geniza. Mercedes had told Stacy, a professional organizer who'd come to help sort stuff, that the old military trunk was a *geniza*. That was in a pre-quarantine era, another life in a time long ago. Four months ago.

She figured Stacy wouldn't know what a *geniza* was. That was the point. Mercedes is somewhat of a factaholic and she tends to trot out arcane facts when faced with something disturbing, like a trunk packed with family history. Intellectual armor.

A *geniza*? What's that? had come the gratifying question.

A *geniza*, Mercedes had said, is a repository in a synagogue for worn out books and old papers to be thrown away. Originally a Hebrew verb meaning 'to hide' or 'put away.' Then it became a noun. Etymological identity transformation.

Etymological identity transformation! Had she really said something so pretentious? Probably. Shades of Gertrude trying to sound smart. Although not a phrase Gertrude would have known or memorized.

Doesn't make sense to store things you're going to throw out, Stacy had said.

Mercedes should have let it go at that, but oh no, she had to go on to explain that any piece of paper containing the name of God had to be kept until it could receive a proper burial. And on and on to say that the idea was to preserve good things from harm and bad things from harming. And, what's more, the famous *geniza* in Cairo was said to be protected by scorpions and a poisonous snake. And that every seven years the contents of the *geniza* would be taken out and buried.

At least she'd stopped short of telling Stacy that the Hebrew root word was also used for human burial. That within the semantic field of *geniza*, dead texts and dead bodies lie in such close proximity that they're indistinguishable.

Close proximity... dead texts... Oh! The tiles! The mismatched tiles she'd cemented askew along the rim of the kitchen counter. Gifts from people who came to visit over the years from different cities, towns, and countries. Each tile bears the story of a place, a friendship, a lover. Fragments of a life mortared onto a wall. What to do about the tiles?

What to do about the bold, slant-eyed leopard tile from Claudia? Big sensual Claudia from North Carolina who wrote erotic stories about her lover's foot fetishism and even weirder predilections. She could write really good sex. She must be well into her eighties by now. Probably still has a man in her bed and writes about it.

Aqui vive un estillista. You're not a hairdresser, Sherry had said, but you are part Mexican and I wanted to bring you a tile from Puerto Rico. Not that Puerto Rico is Mexico. That's just where I happened to be, and they speak Spanish. Sherry delighted in giving presents!

A leaping rabbit from Deborah, abstract patterns from Michael and Caitlin, her translation buddies. They used to meet every month to critique their work, usually at Mercedes's. It's been a while. New Yorkers are so busy. Chisel the leopard, the *estillista*, the rabbit, and so many others out of their cemented settings? And do what with them?

Greek statues were fettered to their pedestals, their stone wings clipped out of fear they would abandon their cities during periods of crisis. Nonetheless, cities were destroyed, statues and lives shattered. Fetters bend and flex, wings flutter. Confines and genealogies are re-mapped. Rivers change their course. The orange segment that marks The Zone in a 1957 Hammond's Complete World Atlas is invalidated.

Guests used to feel at home in her apartment, whether for a drink or a weekend. She didn't fuss, left it to them to uncork a wine bottle, make a bed or a cup of coffee, come and go as they pleased. Shopping yes, she shopped. Soy milk for Cheryl, expresso coffee for Linda, Earl Grey tea for Eduardo. Shelter. She gave them shelter. A home away from home.

They, in turn, pried her away from books and computer. It was Sherry who took her to the museum of perfumes near Carnegie Hall. Mercedes hadn't known it existed. They dipped their noses into rows of little white cubicles, like pecking chickens. Inhale. Aaah, oh! Ugh, too sweet. Wow! Fern and Sally got Mercedes to performances at La Mama, St. Ann's Warehouse, Signature. Katia and Salem led her to out-of-the-way restaurants. Salem introduced her to the Ethiopian place right around the corner. The spongy injera bread was unlike anything Mercedes had ever eaten. What's it made of, she'd asked. Just water, salt, and teff. Teff? It's a grain called love grass back home, Salem explained. Mercedes found the injera tasteless but was glad to consume a grain called love.

Art exhibitions too. Martha introduced her to Zarina Hashmi's drawings and woodcuts. Zarina Hashmi! Floor plans of homes and maps of cities and borders, new and old, penciled, inked, pierced, scratched, cut into being, overlaid with lines of Urdu calligraphy, Zarina's native tongue. All places where the artist once lived: Aligharh, Bangkok, Tokyo, Paris, New York . . . Many drawings so small they'd easily fit in a handbag.

Two days ago Mercedes read the obituary in the paper. The intensity of her grief was unexpected. Zarina Hashmi. Eighty-two. Complications of Alzheimer's. Homes in a handbag ... Corpses in body bags ...

But all that—perfumes and exotic food and art and theater—was a while ago. Why had she become such a recluse long before mandated quarantine? Was it that she strained to keep her wits about her in company? Being part of even the friendliest conversation among friends became an exertion, a depletion. Alone, nobody sees your slipups. Nobody to know you put the phone in the refrigerator, left the chicken out overnight and had to throw it in the garbage, left the apartment keys dangling outside the front door. Nobody to know you forgot the eggs you'd set to boil. Nobody to see the scorched pan, see the egg whites, crusty yolks, and pink shells splattered all over cabinets and floor. Nobody to smell the stench of burn and rotten stink.

Oh! She must remember the chicken soup simmering overnight in the crockpot. Organic, healthy, bland. Nothing like the soup Holly made when Mercedes came down with the flu after flying home from a conference in Chicago. A soup delicious like no other: mushrooms, peppers, lots of herbs, garlic and onions, and more than a dash of hot sauce. A soup full of spices and surprises, like Holly herself.

Mercedes hasn't kept in touch. It's been … how many years? Is she still alive? Diane and Azra and Craig have all died. Cancer and AIDS. It's been years since she's spoken with the cousins, Aunt Lola's gangly redhead boys, now balding men. Her only living next of kin.

She scans the kitchen. Colorful orange cabinets. Pots hang on bent nails alongside strands of deep red peppers and ropes of pale purple garlic; oranges and avocados fill a bright green bowl; more bowls of various sizes, patterns, and colors stack on counters; bananas suspend from a hook; a splattered apron drapes over a chair. All is just like Inmaculada's kitchen.

Things, objects, goods, paraphernalia. Tangible, hands-on stuff. The etymologist Henry Fox-Talbot thought it probable that "thing" originally meant "word," from the German *Ding*, hence the old Latin *dingua*. Thus, he concluded, any thing is an anythink. Mercedes had tried to follow his train of associations. She got as far as the derivatives of *ding* and found only Icelandic, Swedish, Danish, and Old Norse significations of striking, banging, beating—not Latin and nothing to do with thinking.

She regrets having researched the word. No matter. She'll still believe she's surrounded by anythinks. She has a special fondness for Fox-Talbot's travels along trains of association right or wrong. For him, a shadow thrown across a path was enough to set in motion a queue of related thoughts. (It amuses her to think of his interlocking speculations as "queues," appropriate for the British landed-gentleman that he was.) Such queues led him to become one of the first inventors of photography. Mercedes has never been driven to arrive at practical conclusions; she never could have invented photography. It's the thoughts in and of themselves, the impractical flow of one to another that she finds compelling—the way an idea will drift into a new environment, adapt to it, be transformed by it. Like the anythinks that drift into her home. Her belongings.

When her possessions no longer have a life of recollections beyond themselves, the time will have come. For now, her life, her quarantined life, is still rich in memories.

≈ ECOFACTS

The floppy pink rhinoceros that the child, Katie, gave her is nestled on her bed. You need a lovey, she'd said. Mercedes hugs it next to her as she fumbles for an issue of *Harper's* on the side table. She always reads before sleep to clear her mind. A review of a conference on "The Chicken: Its Biological, Social, Cultural, and Industrial History from Neolithic Middens to McNuggets." Middens? What the hell are middens? She gets out of bed to look up the word. Aha! Middens: an ancient garbage dump containing ecofacts associated with human occupation. Ecofacts! Her belongings—everyone's belongings—will become ecofacts should planet earth endure in some form. A vase, a letter, a kitchen tile, a book, even a turd—all ecofacts. What might a future archeologist make of them?

She turns off the light. ...bell pebble ...old atlas...old trunk . . . yellow vase... She falls asleep murmuring echoing names of ecofacts to be discovered in some distant time, traces of a life long extinct.

. . . behind thick glass walls of the lounge jets ascend and descend . . . the plane is lumbering toward departure . . . ghostly bodies press against glass walls ... Gertrude flutters a hand ... César thrusts a fist ... goodbye . . . goodbye . . . Luisa sways adios, *te cuides, Mercedes, te cuides.* Take care. Inmaculada stands tall, cleaver in hand, a broad smile on her face.

. . . Mercedes drifts down down down the vortex of a tropical gyre. Did gyre and gimbal in the wabe ... scraps of disintegrating photographs float by . . . fragments of a long gray submarine . . . bits of a map . . . shards of kitchen tiles . . . pictures curl away from a scrapbook... swollen pages of books loosen from spinal moorings. . . words caught in swaying sea-weeds water-drift to illegibility. Scraps of lost signifiers caught among oscillating sea plants brush against her bare flesh, tender aquatic neurons connecting and disconnecting, welcoming her to their world.

Memories of a future.

STORIES: ENVIORONMENTAL AND OTHER LAPSES

ENVIRONMENTAL LAPSES

≈ HIS AND HERS

Taped above the counter in his kitchen is a small, tattered photograph of a man and a woman standing against a backdrop of mountains. The woman was his wife, long deceased. Breast cancer. She is in profile, turned towards him. He looks directly at the camera.

Since his retirement as a NASA scientist, he spends most of his time in his kitchen which doubles as a sitting room. There is an easy chair covered with a red and black plaid blanket, a wood-burning stove, a small TV, a radio, and a brown wooden shelf stacked with books: *The Microbiology of Food Fermentation*, *The Chelsea Whistle* (a woman's raunchy coming-of-age story), *Raised on Radio* (in 1940s and '50s), *An Introduction to Linear Algebra and Tensors*, *The Metaphysical Club* (19th-century New England intellectuals), *Will You Miss Me When I'm Gone?* (Carter family singing group).

On the wall next to the stove hangs a large photograph of a motel in which it is possible to make out the small figure of a woman seated in front of one of the doors. He took the picture. The woman is a former secretary. They were on a business trip. They did not have an affair, although he wished they'd had.

Upstairs, in a back room he never uses, a framed photograph of his wife in a wedding dress is propped on a dresser. It was taken on the occasion of her marriage to her first husband.

Photographs of his mother, his brothers, his only son are stuffed in a kitchen drawer along with pictures of friends.

≈

In her kitchen the refrigerator door is crowded with magnetized pictures of smiling faces: her grown son now living abroad, a favorite uncle in a rose garden, a beloved aunt, and friends who hug and mug for the camera. She has a miniscule TV in the kitchen that she rarely watches. Two straight-backed chairs on either side of a red Formica table are the only places to sit. The books in her kitchen are all on cooking.

Those she is reading are piled on her bedside table. *The Chelsea Whistle*, a gift from him, is on top. Other books would be of little interest to him: *Thirteen Ways of Looking; History: A Novel*; *Crimes of Writing: Problems in the Containment of Representation, Collected Poems of Emily Dickinson*. A possible exception is *The Stories of Vladimir Nabokov*.

Two more photographs of her son are taped onto a mirror in her bedroom. On the dresser below is a picture of her mother standing between her son and herself. All three are smiling, their arms around each other. It was taken when her mother no longer recognized them. Nearby are photographs of two grandmothers and one grandfather, the one who was still alive when she was a child. Photographs of her father, long absent in her life, are stuffed in a box on a high closet shelf jammed alongside pictures of her son's father, who walked out on her after twenty years of marriage.

≈

His suburban house is dark, hemmed in by trees that he refuses to fell or trim. The walls are the soft brown of neglect marked by a few pale rectangles where paintings once hung.

The sparkling white walls of her city apartment are punctuated by colorful oils and pastels illuminated by light streaming through windows high above the park across the street. In her home are many plants and two cats.

Nothing grows or moves in his house aside from the flicker of a computer or television screen and the slow motion of his body as he methodically dresses, prepares a meal, and wends himself through the hours of the day.

He is uneasy in her home. It is too bright, too clean, too busy. She is oppressed by his house. It is too dark, too dusty, too silent, too full of absence.

≈

Nonetheless. He and she are lovers, drawn to one another by the need for a smile and a glance that is not fixed within a photograph, the need for a touch that is of flesh, not celluloid, the need for a voice not bound within a printed page or merely remembered, but one that vibrates in the present. In the duskiness of his house she embraces him next to a window where shafts of light flicker through the branches of trees. In the lightness of her home he lowers his head to the curve of her neck and shoulder, nestling within the shade of her long dark hair.

≈

Do you know, he writes, *that the relationship between the instant Environmental Lapse Rate (ELR) and the Adiabatic Lapse Rate (ALR) determines whether a parcel of air will sink, stay where it is, or rise to form updrafts and clouds? In short,* he explains, *it determines the stability of the atmosphere.* That's his lead into saying he can't continue the relationship, not even sporadically as has been their pattern. *Too destabilizing,* he adds, as if she wouldn't get the metaphor.

An email. Not an old fashioned hand-written letter where the pressure of pen on paper leaves a tangible trace of a body like the trail of a worm in the dust. She checks the delete box. Hesitates. Checks the garbage icon. The message vanishes into thin air.

THE LEAP

She has to move, stride away the pain of his rejection. In the noon heat she speed-walks across Central Park. Her cotton tee shirt and pants dampen with sweat and cling to her body.

On the far side of the park she trots up the steps to the museum. The blast of air conditioning cools the sweat on her face. It tickles as it dries. The guards examine the purse she'd grabbed on her way out. They fail to notice the sharp shards of a breakup and move her on by.

She wanders among rooms of hangings blindly walking by landscapes, cityscapes, festivities, portraits. Until a photograph stops her short. A pair of legs dangle from the top margin of the picture, high above a cityscape. Pin-striped trousers, crisply creased, cover the legs; the feet are shod in elegant soft leather. One leg is bent at the knee, the other thrusts forward as if kicking.

A suicide, she thinks. He has leapt from a great height. She turns to the wall label: *The Photographer* by Willi Ruge, 1931. He snapped it during a seven-minute parachute jump from an airplane over Berlin. Despite the protests of friends, she reads, Willi risked his life for this vertiginous image.

Not quite a suicide, but a flirtation with death. For seven minutes Willi, elegantly dressed, deliberately suspended himself in the atmosphere between life and death. He would live another thirty years after this leap downwards into the houses and streets and gardens of his native Berlin dimly visible in the photograph. He was almost eighty when he died of natural causes.

FRAGILE X

She sits on an orange plastic chair in the cramped waiting room, breasts naked under a blue hospital gown. She thinks of her former lover's dead wife whose wedding picture to a former husband he kept in an unused room. She wonders if she too will die of cancer and if he will keep a photograph of her and where.

An elderly volunteer, Ethel according to her I.D. tag, has put her clothes—her waist-up clothes and coat, that is—in one of the narrow metal lockers that line a wall of this room of anxious anticipations. Ethel has forgotten to snap shut the padlock to the locker. It dangles, as open and vulnerable to assault as are the nearby breasts awaiting diagnosis.

She has forgotten this simple task because she is absorbed in talking about her thirty-five-year-old daughter with breast cancer. A daughter who had a mastectomy and then an eruption of cancer at the location of the absent breast. It is not a story the five women in their identical blue gowns want to hear. She considers reporting Ethel to a supervisor for further job training.

She turns away, twisting herself sideways to avoid eye contact with the volunteer. She's reminded of children afflicted by the developmental syndrome poetically named Fragile X. Fragile Xs have an extreme aversion to looking at faces, contorting themselves to circumvent a glance.

She thinks of the little pink plastic Xs that will soon be placed on her nipples and along the scar on the side of her left breast, a breast become smaller than the one on the right. That tumor was not malignant. Will she be so lucky this time? Breast cancer killed her exuberant grandmother. She had had a mastectomy, like the volunteer's daughter, and then another until there was nothing left to take except her life. Morphine, a deliberate overdose.

On a TV screen on a wall, people are dying of some rare African disease. Pretend deaths from a pretend disease on an episode of General Hospital. The programming, she thinks, could use some adjusting along with the volunteer. Then a real threat interrupts the pretend one. The mayor of New York takes over the screen to announce that the anthrax poisoning that has made headlines is merely an isolated case. He tells the five women in blue gowns seated in orange plastic chairs in front of the TV that the patient is in intensive care, his life hanging by the proverbial thread.

The large woman sitting next to her says she's worried about a lump in one breast. Her Afro is dyed bright red and her lipstick matches her hair. Huge gold hoops dangle from her ears. A skirt of bold floral patterns flares out below the drab hospital gown. Her appearance defies death. She rants against George W. Bush. The war, the economy, the environment, the deceit and stupidity of it all. Anger over someone who is not in any immanent danger of dying is a strange comfort.

The woman's name is called. She heaves herself up. Good luck, she says.

Good luck to you too.

As brief as their encounter has been, she feels a loss. They will never know each other's fate. She pulls out her note-pad, jots a few lines. Maybe one day she'll write this woman's story. She'll write her as a survivor.

Her name is called. Her turn.

It's Friday. The tests will be analyzed on Monday and the results sent to her doctor in a week. Back in the dressing room she peels off the pink Xs pasted on her breasts, puts on bra and camisole and sweater and coat. Layered against the winter cold, she will keep fragility at bay as she steps out of the hospital into the sharp sunshine of a life.

BLIND DATE

Alfredo and Gloria have invited her to dinner along with a Museum Director, a Divorced Museum Director, they tell her. Your type. She checks him out on the internet. He exists in cyber space. There is even a photograph.

She tries not to get her hopes up, inhaling deeply the scent of the bound incense sticks she keeps on her desk (she's read that frankincense calms mice), but the photograph throws her off balance. He has put on a nice open smile for the camera. A gentle spirit, she thinks, although years of editing photographs and countless blind dates have taught her that photographs can be supremely deceptive. And yet a few fantasies drift through her mind when she isn't monitoring her thoughts.

Waking on the morning of the day of the dinner she rolls over and reaches for him, imagining the sweet photo smile greeting her, imagining strong arms tenderly circling her shoulders, imagining a gentle kiss, lips not yet tainted by the day's speaking. Then she catches herself, rises abruptly, makes the bed, shaking out the sheets and drawing them tight, smoothing over the phantom presence of the man she has yet to meet.

AL DENTE

At the small round table, they seat her next to the Divorced Museum Director. A Russian curator dressed like a hooker is to the other side of him, and next to her a gay Greek journalist who arrived late. The hosts have placed themselves between two Italian women artists. Their art is conceptual, mostly installations.

Gloria, Alfredo's new, much younger girlfriend, is nervous.

"The risotto is excellent," she assures Gloria, "perfectly al dente."

Gloria gives a sigh of relief. "You really like it?"

"Yes, I really do."

"I cook potatoes al dente," says the Divorced Museum Director. "It's very difficult to cook potatoes al dente. Most potatoes are too mushy."

Alfredo agrees that potatoes, like pasta and rice, should be al dente.

"What's your secret for al dente potatoes?" she asks the Divorced Museum Director. It's early in the evening. She's still holding on to the memory of his smile on her computer screen.

The computer smile is quickly replaced by a what-a-stupid-question look on his unsmiling face. "I'm a vegetarian.

That's how I know how to cook vegetables. I eat fish, but not salmon. I hate salmon."

"The paté is salmon," Alfredo informs him.

"I didn't have any. I hate paté. All that stuff mashed together, the geese force-fed, tubes down their throats. It's like bad sex."

"I like meat," she declares, although she's not a big meat-eater. "I often crave meat," she insists.

The Divorced Museum Director wiggles in closer to her. "Just to hear you say that makes me all tingly."

BILL OF HEALTH

"A clean bill of health," the doctor tells her over the phone.

She ponders the expression. Why not a clean invoice of health? Clean tab of health? Why the association with what is usually a demand for payment? A reminder of the other kind of bill that she knows will soon be in the mail? Yes, she will pay for this statement, pay the statement, but not with her life. Only money, more and more for her clean-bill health as she grows older.

If her breasts were riddled with cancer cells would he have called her into his office, and said, in the requisite mournful intonation, "Sorry to inform you, but you have a dirty bill of health"?

In the morning she turns on the shower, getting the temperature just right. Stepping under the rushing water, she slowly lathers her breasts with perfumed soap.

ALL CLEAR

When the phone rings she's watching one of her favorite detective programs. She doesn't recognize the number, but on the third peal she decides to take the call, muting the TV, still keeping her eyes on the corpse, silent to begin with, and on the homicide detectives now merely mouthing directives.

It's the Divorced Museum Director. She hadn't given him her number. He must have gotten it from Alfredo.

"How about dinner Saturday?" he barks.

"I'm not free on Saturday."

"What about Sunday?"

"Sunday's no good either."

"Popular woman," he snaps.

"Yes."

"Well then, up to you. You know where to find me."

"Right." She hangs up quickly, avoiding infection.

The three policemen on the TV screen enter the apartment of a suspect, room by room, guns in hand. She turns the sound back on.

"Clear," the first shouts.

"Clear," shouts the second.

"Clear now," says the third.

DESCENT

In a room on the twenty-first floor, a scholar at a podium is pontificating on Italy's North/South disputation. He stands squarely, his back to a floor-to-ceiling window. A black man dangles aloft outside, washing the wide expanse of glass. He, the man outside, is sheathed in blue overalls, the same blue as the vast immensity of sky behind him. The scholar inside is unaware of the man outside who hovers above his head, a being whose strokes bring the sky to luminous clarity. The man descends—a cleansing swoop behind the scholar's head, behind his neck, his chest, behind the podium. A final swirl outside at floor level coincides with the scholar's inside summation: Calabria is equal to Africa. The window washer drops out of sight.

WHAT DO YOU FEEL?

I was persuaded, if not coerced, to join a group therapy session. My boss was concerned about my mental well-being. I panic when I have to speak in a setting with more than two other people. I rarely utter a word during meetings unless obliged to give a report or am asked a question. On these occasions, I flush bright red from my face down to my neck and chest. I jumble words. My discomfort is highly visible and audible. It was the Human Resources therapist/social worker, part-time hire to do assessments and recommendations for employees in psychic angst, who proposed group therapy. Group Therapy! A room full of strangers discussing personal traumas. I flushed at the mere thought. He insisted, in that pseudo soft voice that bad therapists adopt, he insisted the experience would be helpful to overcome my shyness in public. The group he proposed was small and intimate. Sessions took place in the therapist's apartment. Cozy, non-threatening environment, he assured me.

The sessions were run by Olga. She emailed me the rules beforehand. Never arrive late. Never arrive more than five minutes early. Shoes off by the door. No food or drink, not even water. No socializing with any member of the group. Should you happen to run into one of them, do not engage in any discussion beyond the weather. In fact, do not discuss anything that goes on in the group with anyone. That would dilute The

Process. Never reveal the circumstances under which you came to know the group member.

Olga's apartment is lush, creamy, and overstuffed. She is an ample tall blonde of an equally ample age she would probably not admit to. She's swathed in a flowing beige tunic and is fully shod (albeit in elegant slippers) unlike us barefoot or sock-wearing damaged creatures. She sits in a highbacked armchair, turned away from the big windows giving out onto a park in full foliage. We penitents sit on metal folding chairs semi-circling out from her throne. The hour is one that many people consider dinner time. Olga is one of them. A tray with a full platter of sushi is on her lap. She chopsticks each morsel and dips it liberally in a dish of soy sauce. At intervals she sips from a mug that one would assume contained tea although, with Olga, no rules seem to apply.

Joan talks about a recent blind date. She was excited to meet the man mainly because, like her, he is a vegetarian. "Not easy to find," she says.

"I blew it," she moans. "I told him I had been a member of a Buddhist group for twenty years. He got up and left and that's the last I heard of him."

There is a long silence while we all look at Joan sympathetically and then, as the silence wears on, down at our hands resting on our laps. How prolonged can a sympathetic look be? How long can we sit looking at our hands? I glance sideways at Olga, whose mouth is full of sushi, then back at Joan who is looking down, fingering her hands. Her long dark hair partially curtains her face.

Silence. Not one of stillness and calm. Not speechless shock. A silence of uncertainty, of waiting, that becomes a form of torture. I hear someone speak. It's my voice. I am the one speaking.

"I don't think you blew it. Saying you belong to a Buddhist group is part of who you are. Nothing to be sorry for."

Olga swallows her morsel of sushi and asks me, "How do you feel, Janet, saying that?"

"I think…"

"Not what you *think*, Janet. What do you *feel?*"

"I felt badly for Joan since nobody was saying anything."

"And how do you *feel*, Joan, having Janet say what she just said?"

Joan shrugs, "I think maybe she cares."

"Not *think*, Joan, do you *feel* that Janet cares?"

"I guess so."

Olga looks around the room. "What does anyone else *feel* about what Janet said to Joan?"

Another long silence.

Joe says, "I feel Janet was condescending."

"Aha!" exclaims Olga waving her chopsticks in the air. "Now we're getting somewhere. Getting to something neither Janet or Joan can admit."

"I thought, that is, I *felt*, I was trying to make Joan feel better," I say.

"You were being superior, Janet. You made her feel worse."

"I don't feel worse," Joan says.

"Oh, you will," says Olga as she pinches another piece of sushi.

My folding chair clangs as I get up to leave. I smile at Joan, grab my shoes by the door, and wait outside on the chance Joan will follow. She does not. I can only hope she hasn't started to feel worse.

THEY WILL WAKE YOU IN THE MORNING

"The crows will wake you in the morning," he'd said.

But they didn't.

Grief woke her as it had every morning for the past month. Coming into wakefulness on a bed in a crumbling villa, she felt the sting of tears behind her closed eyelids. It was only later she heard the cawing. A single crow, a cry far away, a harsh sound softened by distance, softened by leaves rustling on a tree near the window where she lay in ruins.

The night before they'd dined on a high terrace that overlooked an expanse of fields and mountains beyond the fields. The terrace projected out into the landscape with merely the crumbled remains of what had been a protective balustrade.

No place for a child, she'd thought. But there was no child.

The man, a man she had not known until the day before, slept deeply unaware of the single crow crying in the distance.

PAINLESS

The dog was licking her face. A furry black dog. It was dark. How long had she been lying on the pavement? It had been daylight when she fell. That she remembers. She crawled over cobblestones and gravel, the dog ahead, barking. That she remembers. Then whiteness. Space of no memories. Ambulance. Her mother bending over her. Can you hear me, hear me, hear me!

Was it the next day that someone brought her two orange fish in a round bowl? She remembers them swimming in and out of her mind's whiteness as she lay cranked to a tilt on a bed as white as her mind. Watery black eyes stared, slithery mouths gulped open. Did she scream? The orange fish were soon disappeared.

≈

Her mother was folding clothes into a suitcase, a suitcase that smelled of newness. She was fourteen and being packed away to boarding school, disappeared like the gulping goldfish. It was then, seven years after the fall, that her mother, smoothing a new blue sweater into a new brown valise—it was then that her mother said, stop crying, you're lucky to be alive, you almost died in that accident.

≈

Now she watches her own child scrambling up a slide in the playground holding tight its silvery edges. She has a startling memory of not having held on to the rusty rails of that long-ago fire escape, of having leaned into the fall, of having given herself up to it. Not because of a will to die, but because of an absence of a will to live.

She closes her eyes trying to conjure a memory of pain. The pain immediately after the fall or the pain that must have sliced its way through the drugs in the hospital. Nothing. Her breath comes in and out of her lungs, her belly expands and subsides, but she can't remember the pain, only the horror of the staring, gulping fish.

Back home from the playground, her little girl tucked safely in bed, she goes to the computer. She types: memory and pain. Site after site is about the short-term memory of pain, not the long-term forgetting of it. The newsletter of the International Association for the Study of Pain is no help.

Yet the search has its rewards. She learns about nerves that carry pain signals to the spinal cord and brain to excite the cells that make memories of pain—a cellular excitation that produces an heightened reactivity to pain that can last for months. Her cells must have been revved up, excited, sensitive to a pain she can no longer recall.

"Excite" a technical term. Yes, but she pictures a nervy little creature bringing a message of pain to a nebbish looking cell.

"Yo man, belly just sliced open like a sausage. Blood spurting everywhere. What a scene! Hurts like hell."

"Wow! Cool. Tell me more. Hold on, lemmy grab a pencil and paper."

She learns about molecules called ERKs—extracellular signal-related kinases—that can change the memory of cells in the spinal cord and brain. Molecular psychotherapy! She reads up on the marine snail Aplysia that is very attractive to neurobiologists because of large brain cells that are up to one millimeter in diameter. One millimeter! What is the size of a human brain cell? She hasn't a clue. She logs out, shuts down her computer.

She calls her friend Richard whose store of knowledge is phenomenal and who was once married to a doctor. "Memory is not intended to be an archive," he tells her. "We have an automatic extinguishing mechanism that remembers having the pain but not the pain itself. Otherwise we could not go on." That makes sense. Except for certain phobias and an intense dislike of oatmeal Richard usually makes sense.

It is reassuring to know that, even if her brain cells turn out to be smaller than those of a mollusk, her pain extinguishing mechanism is working in full force.

Tomorrow she and her daughter will make up a story about a brainy snail named Aplysia. A snail who feels no pain. A joyous snail with a will to live.

TOP SECRET

"Water."

The April day too bright blue glorious to refuse, Tomoko and I have left the gray confines of the International School and are standing alongside a pond in a nearby park.

"Water," I repeat. Tomoko looks at me in polite bewilderment. I'm surprised she doesn't know the word, even given the limitations of her vocabulary—limitations she's straining to overcome.

"Restaurant," I say. That's a word I know she knows. Tomoko eats out a lot with her boyfriend Harry, an American. I'd hoped he'd improve her English, but Tomoko's told me he does all the talking.

"She likes explain. Very intelligent, Harry," Tomoko says.

"What does Harry explain?" I ask, after reminding her that "she" is for women, for you, Tomoko, and for me, Doreen. "He" is for men, for Harry. Tomoko knows this but gender designations are slippery for her, in English at least.

"Harry talk very fast. Maybe I not understand."

Tomoko's English is sprinkled with "maybes." It's a word that seems to have multiple meanings for her despite our looking up its Japanese equivalent in the little electronic dictionary she carries in her purse. Or perhaps it's just a fallback word when she isn't sure she's understood a question.

"What is Harry's job?" I hesitate to ask, worried that I'm prying and unsure of getting an answer. Aside from telling me he takes her to restaurants, Tomoko has not been forthcoming about Harry.

"Maybe lawyer," Tomoko tells me.

He likes explain. I suspect corporate law.

I point again at the pond. "Water. Waiter comes: 'Glass of water?'" I mimic drinking.

"Water," Tomoko repeats. She's got it.

"Ducks." I point.

"Yes, ducks," Tomoko affirms, nodding. Her hair—cut shaggy just above her shoulders—is so black it glitters blue in the sun. I suspect she knows "duck" from restaurant menus. A vision of a crisp carcass on Harry's dinner plate overlays the sight of emerald-feathered fowl trailing ripples and quacks across the smooth surface of the pond. I hold Harry responsible for the indefensible murder of all ducks.

We continue our walk, Tomoko balancing easily on high-heeled boots. With every step, black rayon shimmers over taut muscles. She was a high school gym teacher in Japan. In New York, she goes to the gym nearly every day. At forty, she has the flat-chested, skinny body of a teenager, only without the awkwardness. She learned the word "dolphin" at Equinox. The lifeguard told her, "You're a dolphin, that's what you are. A dolphin!" I picture her in a black tank suit effortlessly skimming the water, quick rise of buttocks as she executes somersault turns at the end of each lap.

I learned to swim late in life. After the ending of my twenty-five year marriage, I was having recurring dreams of drowning and the university where I taught offered free lessons to staff. I barely managed the crawl, never attempting upside down turns. Since retirement, I just splash a bit in the ocean the few summer days I get out of town. I won't drown, but I never was and never will be a dolphin.

I continue to point. "Tree . . . branch . . . leaf . . ."

"Flowers," I say and then, "crocuses, daffodils." Not useful words for a beginner, but the newly emerged blossoms flirt for specification.

"I love flower. In Japan I make Ikebana."

"Ikebana flower arrangements?"

"Yes. I study long time Ikebana." Tomoko turns to me, smiling. "Suisen."

"Suisen?" It's my turn for perplexity.

"Daffodil in Japanese," she explains. "Suisen."

"Suisen," I repeat, savoring the softness of the "s's". "Suisen," I whisper. "Like telling a secret," I say to Tomoko.

"Suisen—top secret," she whispers back. I feel the faint flicker of her breath brush my ear.

Tomoko watches DVDs of action movies with Harry and has acquired snippets of phrases from their infrequent moments of dialogue.

We move to a waterfall. I say, "waterfall."

Tomoko's expression of polite bewilderment returns.

"Water."

She nods. I pretend to fall. "Oops!" Then point to the waterfall. "Water fall, waterfall."

Tomoko beams. "Waterfffffalll," she repeats. "F's" are hard for her when they are in the middle of a word. We've spent a lot of time on middle "F's." "Coffee" was the trial word. At Starbucks—her favorite place in the city after the gym—she'd ask for "Cau-hee." "Dolphin" became another practice sound, though with a "ph" and useful only at Equinox. And now daffodils. She learned "F's" by watching me exaggerate them, placing her lower lip in back of her neatly aligned teeth and breathing out with an emphatic "fffff," looking like an anxious beaver.

When I volunteered to be a Conversation Partner, I was given a chart with drawings of lips, tongues, and teeth, but immediately put it aside. It seemed too personal, even pornographic, and at the same time too clinical. Months of attempted conversation with Tomoko have taught me that some people can't hear pronunciation. Tomoko is someone who has to see pronunciation. I am intimately aware of the movements of our mouths and tongues. I'm always sure to apply lip-gloss and floss my teeth before we meet.

"Waterfffffalll . . . Waterfffffalll," Tomoko repeats. We laugh. We laugh a lot. I've read that all language groups laugh 'ha-ha-ha' basically the same way. Each 'ha' is about one-fifteenth of a second. Faster or slower than that and it sounds more like panting or, the article said, "something else." Our 'ha-ha-ha's' must be one-fifteenth of a second because they always sound like laughter.

Hearing and sight are not essential to laughter. Deaf people laugh. Blind people laugh. People on phones laugh. Tomoko and I don't laugh on the phone. We never talk on the phone—too difficult for her. Email is our only other viable mode of communication and any laughter by that means would not be simultaneous.

Email may soon be our only means of communication. Unless Tomoko can get her visa extended, she'll be going back to Japan in two months.

"I need job. For work visa. My English not good."

"Maybe you marry Harry?"

"No."

Fast-talking Harry. I'm relieved Tomoko doesn't say "maybe." I'm relieved the relationship is not about obtaining a Green Card. What then, is it about? Sex?

Birds chirp. "Birds," I say. "Cheep, cheep, cheep. Sing."

"Birds sing," repeats Tomoko. "Nature DVD." We laugh.

Tomoko's laugh ends abruptly. She looks past my shoulder. "Harry," she says. "I say to him maybe we in park today."

Harry shambles towards us, not the smooth corporate lawyer I expected. He extends a fleshy hand in my direction. "Hiya, you must be Doreen." His complexion is pasty gray in the sunlight, his smile tentative.

I shake the proffered hand, expectedly sweaty. "Why don't we sit," I suggest. "It's a bit awkward to walk and talk with three of us."

"Good idea Doreen." His speech shambles like the rest of him. Is he going to be one of those salesman-like people who repeats your name every other sentence?

We move to a nearby picnic table. Harry and Tomoko sit on one side, I place myself on the other, facing them. They do not touch, have not touched, even in greeting. I feel the absence of sexual frisson, a palpable weight between them.

Harry pulls a leather flask from his hip pocket. "A little something to move the conversation along," he says, then takes a swig. "Want some, Doreen? Don't have any diseases, ha ha." Harry's "ha ha" is not laughter, not one-fifteenth of a second. A something else both aggressive and tentative. I decline, as does Tomoko.

My persistent, unabashed questioning reveals that Harry's job is entering data on a computer in a law firm. How can Tomoko be so deluded? Lovely Tomoko, creator of delicately balanced Ikebana arrangements. I look to her for a sign. Her head is bowed, eyes lowered.

"Tomoko!"

She looks up at me.

"Are you going to the gym today?"

"Maybe."

"She's coming to my place to watch a DVD," Harry asserts.

"No dolphin today?" I say.

Tomoko is silent.

"Dolphin?" asks Harry.

I don't explain. I don't understand why Tomoko is with a man she hasn't told about being a dolphin, with a man whose "ha ha's" aren't laughter. For months, sound waves carrying Harry's incomprehensible explainings have washed over Tomoko. Pollution. Why?

Tomoko is besieged by men. I see how they look at her. And she's shown me a stack of business cards from men at the International School, men on the streets, men at the gym. Bona fide lawyers, corporate executives, art dealers. "Call me. I'll show you around," they say. "Be careful," I advise her.

But Harry? Where did he come from? Why Harry? Harry who doesn't know her as I do? Or does he know her as I don't? Does Harry know a Tomoko I have no idea exists? What have I failed to understand in these months of conversations?

$\approx$

Back home, I pour myself a glass of wine and dig out the bag of nachos I hide in the recesses of a cabinet in the hope I'll forget they are there. Weight never was a problem, but since retirement, I've taken to snacking with predictable dismaying results. Collapsing on the sagging sofa, which I intend to replace someday, I power up the evening news. I watch a lot more TV now that I'm no longer teaching.

A gap-toothed woman with black bangs is wearing a black jacket with a large, viciously pointed white collar. I mute the sound before she has a chance to speak, certain her voice will be as mean as her appearance. She explain. Harry explain. She's being questioned by a square-shouldered man wearing a dark tie with large white polka dots. I wonder what idiot was in charge of wardrobe. Scene cuts to blurry gray footage of gray people wandering disconsolately in a gray rubbled landscape, then cuts again to a dazzling color view of protesters carrying huge signs.

STOP THE BOMBING

In the background a sign spells STOPP. Why two "p's?" What language? Who are these people?

Shift to a naked man, face hooded in black, dense black hair covering his chest, genitalia pixilated—technological fig leaf.

More protesters. STOP TORTURE. Yes, stop torture. A position I understand. Finally, something I understand.

Fast cut to different people carrying more signs, this time in French. ... RENDEZ-VOUS ... EN FIN DE DROIT ... The brief moment of comprehension vanishes. What is this about? What's the point? What rendez-vous? Where? What bombing? Harry explain. Ha ha!

The latest announcer looks French. He has a lot of hair and is not the type to sport a polka dot tie. Flash to the handsome French prime minister, but without his glamorous wife, the one who has to live up or down to the glamorous men she's slept with. In the foreground, a dazzling woman with a short haircut like mine, but dyed a flamboyant red. She's speaking. In French? I understand French. I reach for the remote to turn on the sound, but before my finger touches the button the red-haired woman is replaced by what looks to be a commercial showing a frizzy-furred monkey chewing on a huge, overly bright green leaf. I don't understand monkeys. I power off the TV. STOPP!

Tears tickle down my cheeks. Waterfall. Waterfffffalll. Water fall. Oh Tomoko, how could you? Harry explain. STOPP. What is this world coming to?

≈

The phone rings while I'm having breakfast. It's 7:30. I figure a drowsy person or a clueless politician in another time zone dialed the wrong number so I let it go. Then change my mind and pick up on the fourth peal.

"I am Tomoko."

"Tomoko! Are you OK?"

"OK. I want to speak to you. I want to come to your apartment."

"Yes. When?"

"OK now? I am in lobby."

"OK now."

Tomoko is wearing a form-fitting white sweater, a black and white ruffled mini skirt, black leggings, and a pair of silvery ballerina shoes. I am in a tatty, baby-blue, chenille bathrobe that, like the sofa, I've been meaning to replace.

"Gift," she says, still standing by the front door. She hands me a small green box. "Tea. Green tea."

"Thank-you. Please, come in."

She remains at the door. "How you like Harry?" she asks. The question rushes into a single word: hayouliharry.

I take a deep breath, then make a so-so gesture with my right hand, palm up palm down. She repeats my gesture. It must be international code.

I translate into English. "So-so," I say.

"Me too. So-so."

She follows me into the kitchen where I brew the tea she's brought. We sit at the little red Formica table and wait for it to steep. Out of a labor intensive narrative on Tomoko's part, I learn she was introduced to Harry by an older Japanese friend who extolled his virtues.

"She friend of my mother and father," Tomoko explains.

I slowly come to understand how, brought up to obey her elders, Tomoko has been obediently striving to see what Harry's virtues might be, thinking herself a failure for not perceiving them. It is her first time outside of Japan, her first immersion in another culture and a foreign language. It all begins to make sense.

She tells me she had sex only once with Harry, weeks ago. I'm not surprised by the fact, but by the revelation. Up to this moment, apart from restaurants and DVDs, Tomoko has been guarded about her relationship with Harry. I take a slow sip of tea and remind myself that I too am an elder who should be heeded. In the most comprehensible, delicate, and forceful terms I can muster, I assure her Harry is a jerk.

"Tomoko, you are wonderful. You can find a good man, a man better than Harry. Harry is not a good man."

"I think so. But I need to speak good English."

"Then we will study very, very hard."

"Yes, study very hard."

"Have you told Harry?"

"No."

"When are you going to tell Harry?"

"Maybe."

Mine a difficult grammatical construction for a Japanese. "When?" I repeat. "Tonight tell Harry? Tomorrow tell Harry? Next week?"

"Oh! I do not know. Maybe. Top secret."

I nod, "Top secret."

Leaving, Tomoko gives me one of her rare and fleeting versions of a hug—barest touch of an arm, soft flick of hair to my cheek.

"Suisen," she whispers.

"Suisen," I whisper back.

DEPARTURES

The husband often travels to a foreign continent on business. There he falls in love with a foreign woman. They have two half-foreign children. His absence on each continent becomes prolonged and multiplied. Kids on two continents rush into his arms. Daddy! Daddy! Papa! Papa! He unpacks gifts from the continent where he is not.

The wife on the first continent, the one who is not foreign, takes up baking. She kneads. She takes up clay modeling and kneads some more. She shapes bowls and vases and loaves of bread. Her hands grow strong and she grows fat. She takes up smoking and kneads ashtrays. A smoldering cigarette ignites a curtain and the house burns down. The wife and children are reduced to ashes and bones. The husband remains on the second continent, the one that was once foreign. He is grateful to have a spare family.

IN A CASTLE IN FRANCE

Once upon a time in a castle in France a man locked his wife in a tower upon learning she had a lover. She lived alone for forty years save for a trusted servant who brought her frugal meals. Apart from a narrow bed, her room was bare. In a moment of pity, the dishonored husband granted her one request. She asked for paints and brushes. So it came to pass that on the gray walls of her cell grew lush green fields sprinkled with red poppies flourishing beneath blue skies flecked with white clouds. Only after her death did the secret heart of her artistry come to light: her bed upturned, its wooden underside revealed a full-bodied portrait of her lover, his bare, young arms reaching to embrace the hard surface on which she had lain those forty years.

MOM HAS A LOVER

Today I found out Mom has a boyfriend. A lover, was what I heard Aunt Judy whisper to Mrs. Alberti—she's our next-door neighbor. Aunt Judy also said that the roses decorating the rim of the wooden toilet seat upstairs—they're the peel-off kind—were stuck on there by Mom's lover. I like the word lover. It's very grownup. It's about sex. I know about sex already. It's like when dogs give piggyback rides, only it's not just dogs. I've started to get a kind of achy feeling down there, sort of like when you have to pee, but nicer. Mom said that's a good sign, and she laughed. It was her secret, grownup laugh. I'm sure it has to do with sex. After I heard about Mom's lover, I waited to pee until I couldn't hold it anymore and then I sat down on the roses that Mom's lover had pressed onto the toilet rim. I let it all go in a rush. It felt good.

GROUND RULES

Establish ground rules starting with your first encounter. Do not to talk to him for more than five minutes. When in a group, address all remarks to others, never to him alone. Avoid accidentally brushing against him, even when there is very little space to maneuver in a crowded restaurant. Never smile at him. Never let on in any way that you are attracted to him.

Take care to critique his work with exactly the same attention you give to that of others. Do not be too harsh or too complimentary, even if the work is very bad or very good.

If he should ask you out on a date, turn him down at least three times. Should he persist, on the first date let him do all the talking. Reveal nothing about yourself. Turn him down twice for the second date and then again let him do all the talking and reveal nothing about yourself. Same for the third, the fourth, and all subsequent dates.

Should you end up in bed, never utter sounds of pleasure or whisper words of endearment.

Never call him. Never invite him to any event, especially if your friends are involved.

Prepare for when he will leave. Stock up on friends, pre-cooked food, liquor, sleeping pills, and extra therapy sessions.

The above preparations should also come in handy should he stick around.

PENANCE

Dear Mother,

For many years I lived far away in a country you could not imagine, speaking a language you could not understand. Every week you wrote me a letter in elegant cursive on light blue paper. You wrote of daily comings and goings in good weather and bad. Of who came to tea or dinner and what the women were wearing, who had a new baby, of flowers newly bloomed in the garden.

Foolishly in love and self-absorbed, I rarely wrote back. Your only child became a stranger.

Now it is you who have gone to a faraway place I cannot imagine. A place without language, without a single word or memory we can share. Returned from abroad, I now write you daily postcards in block letters: I AM HOME AGAIN. I AM YOUR DAUGHTER. I select postcards with pictures of bright sunrises and glowing sunsets. Your clouded blue eyes focus for an unknowing instant on the pieces of cardboard I press into your limp hand. Sunrises and sunsets and words slip onto the white sheets of your raised, nursing-home bed.

I write knowing there will be no answer, just as you once wrote me.

Lucy

Dear Mother,

Pardon my wobbly handwriting. I'm on a subway headed for the hospital where you were taken an hour ago. A nice young doctor on the phone told me you were vomiting blood. It is the same hospital where you worked as a secretary between unfortunate marriages.

I will be there soon.

Lucy

Dear Mother,

I write as I sit beside your bed. You lie with your mouth open. A thin trickle of drool drips down one side of your jaw. I can't bring myself to wipe it away. Your wrinkled arm slumps on the white sheet. When I touch your liver-spotted hand you moan.

Lucy

Dear Mother,

The nice young doctor tells me to return you to the nursing home where hospice will starve you to death. No food or drink, just the tip of a sponge to moisten your lips. It should take about three days for you to die, he says. I cry for the first time since his phone call. They did the same for my grandmother, he adds.

Lucy

Dear Mother,

This morning hospice woke me from a medicated sleep: your feet had turned blue. It was just before sunrise when your feet turned blue. When I arrived at your bedside the nurse said you had "passed."

I will place this postcard of a sunrise in your hand for your passage to the crematorium. The one you selected when you were still a sentient being and I was far away. I will write a postcard every week to place on your gravesite. Unspoken words and sunrises and sunsets will crumble, soak into the earth, mingle with your ashes.

Then the day will come when I journey again to a far-away country you could never have imagined, once again speaking a language you never learned.

Love, Lucy

LETTER TO A PAST

A mistake, my carelessness. You came across the photo I'd taken of you in our wicker basket fallen among torn receipts, shredded letters from my mother, drafts of my aborted stories. You held it up to my face sobbing Why? Why?

Two days later you said, "I'm not a virgin anymore," announcing the fact as if you had completed a necessary errand. It's been sixty years and I still see you standing in the doorway of our dorm room. I see you clearly, but in profile. Turning aside? Turning away? From me?

We were sophomores in college. It would be another ten years before your son was born, and both your lives cut short.

≈

Junior year: our shared apartment in Paris. 1965 and our country began bombing Vietnam in earnest. We missed out on the surge of protests back home. In Paris, the Algerian Revolution and its protests had ended. The closest we came to any understanding of Algeria was to read Camus' *The Stranger*. Camus died oh too young and oh so handsome in a car crash, an unused train ticket in his pocket. I slipped a photo of him into my wallet. A cigarette angles from the corner of his mouth. I smoked back then. You never smoked. Only now does it occur to me to ask why. We all smoked. Why not you?

Camus' memoir of his Algerian childhood was smashed away mid-text in the crash and published (in its incompletion) only thirty-five years later. *The First Man.* Whose posthumous title is that? I've yet to read it. I reread *The Stranger*, now in the light of (shadow of?) Kamel Dauod's novel of response. I was innocent of, abysmally ignorant of other perspectives, blanketed in my own traumas and desires, emotionally confused, rebel without a cause. James Dean was my idol, one who, anticipating Camus, died oh too young and oh so handsome in a car crash.

We missed out on the demonstrations, but caught the first wave of the Beatles. Your name song was in the air.

> *Michelle ma belle, Michelle ma belle*
> *Sont des mots qui vont tres bien ensemble*
> *tres bien ensemble*
> *I love you, I love you, I love you*
> *that's all I want to say*
> *Until I find a way...*

Your stolid British boyfriend of that year, Benjamin, and I sang it to you. It didn't matter that neither of us could hold a tune. Other men sang to you too. All infatuated, even my own lover-of-the-year, the medical intern Francis who cheated on me with a nurse then asked me to marry him. I didn't care about the cheating or the proposal. My heart was skipping beats for Blaise, a poet immune to my allure. We were reading Racine, the intensity of Phaedra flooding me—*mad love now deranging me like poison in the blood*—alexandrines orchestrating my despair to heights of passion that, to be honest, I never attained. Sweaty palms waiting for the phone to ring was more like it.

The fervent effect of Racine on my emotions—or at least emotional ambitions—was in part due to the tutelage of Madame Vaudinet who had written a book on him and seemed to know every line of *Phaedre* by heart. But what most heightened the drama was her translucently pale skin, a luminous pallor due, I learned, to a photosensitivity disorder that did not tolerate the slightest ray of sunlight. Sometimes she brought along her little daughter Ondine, a silent wraith hovering in a corner. I attribute Ondine and Madame Vaudinet's ghostly presences to my enthrallment with Racine's fatalism flowing in rhymes of an elegance that even my American accent could not obliterate. You seemed less affected than I was. Or maybe I simply wasn't paying attention.

Madame Vaudinet believed that Racine wrote his plays especially for women's dramatic roles. Portraits of him depict a jowly face loaded down with a heavy wig, black curls cascading onto his shoulders. Yes, it was the fashion of the times, but the depictions only fed my speculation that he, though married with children, might have been gay. My theory was bolstered by the character of Hippolytus, the object of Phaedra's passion, who scorns the love of women. Yes, eventually he is smitten by Aricia, but she is the daughter of his father's enemy, hence forbidden to him. And Hippolytus dies before the possibility of consummation.

My own unconsummated, forbidden amour—thrilling, but more of a dalliance to be honest—consisted of clandestine meetings in the Luxembourg gardens with Professeur Lavoie, a philosopher from the Sorbonne, another conscript to tutor us American girls abroad. (We were all taught individually in keeping with the educational tenents of our progressive college back in the States.) Professeur Lavoie was a pudgy, heavy-lidded, long nosed man who, with the appropriate wig, could have passed for Racine. Nothing like my lover Francis who looked vaguely like James Dean. Nonetheless it was the Professeur who gave new meaning to French kissing, as well as to the ancient Greeks. I admit the kisses made more of a lasting impression than the philosophers. He was not one of your profs and I never told you what was going on. Mostly because you changed the subject at any mention of my love life. As for yours, from what I could tell, dutiful Benjamin seemed to suffice. You were never all-over-the-map-man-crazy like I was, in literature or in the flesh.

Professeur Lavoie would forever remain Professeur Lavoie, first name unknown. Like many French people, he had fixed boundaries and notions of propriety bewildering to a foreigner. He even invited me once for coffee at his dark apartment stuffed with velvet drapes, books, plump furniture, and a plump wife, a mathematics professor. Did I imagine the pitying look she gave me?

Making do with what was available, I went with Francis, on holiday—a week bouncing through the French countryside in his tinny Deux Chevaux. We slept in farmhouses on uncomfortably romantic straw-filled mattresses, woke to roosters crowing the dawn and to lush views of fields and mountains. Once, after our careful *coitus interruptus* (I didn't tell you about that either), I tried out some lines from *Phaedre* (something I doubt you would ever have considered): *Ah, such sweet torture . . . My body burning hot. . .* Francis gave me a concerned look. For a moment I'd forgotten he was a medical intern.

Francis' internship was such that I didn't see much of him in Paris. He was rarely among the French friends we entertained. (We avoided American students.) We cooked on two little burners in the kitchen, a kitchen that was once a closet next to the toilet.

Once I prepared chicken with walnuts. A dish my mother used to make. It did not go over well with the French. So we stuck to the only French recipe we mastered: *coq au vin* simmered in a heavy, blacked pot we bought at a flea market for that purpose. Who got the pot when we left? Did we simply leave it in the apartment? I've never found another quite like it.

We ate in the living room, at our only table, clearing away books and papers onto a corner of the floor to make space. Our apartment was tiny and shabby but its ceilings soared and the French windows with their wrought iron railings of false balconies gave our tight quarters an illusion of expanse and grandeur. I liked to lean out over the balconettes to take in the street scene below, but you were afraid of heights. Our Parisian friends teased us about the word "balconette." It took us a while to figure out that it referred to a type of underwire brassiere in French.

We wanted to speak French and our guests wanted to practice English. Who was it who asked if he should "put the orts in the slop pail"? We had to look up "orts:" late Middle English for food scraps. We thought it ever so funny having to learn Chaucer's English to understand the French.

≈

Ya Mustapha was another song from that year abroad. I imagined a Mustapha with a flowing beard and longing dark eyes, a Muslim for whom I would gladly wear the veil. I sang it to everyone substituting whoever's name it was for Mustapha.

> *Chéri je t'aime chéri je t'adore,*
> *como la salsa de pomodoro.*
> *Y a Mustapha, y a Mustapha*
> *tu m'as allumé avec une allumette*
> *Et tu m'as fait perdre la tête*

Y a Michelle, y a Michelle, I adore you like tomato sauce! Tomato sauce! I'd laugh so hard I usually didn't get to the "set me on fire and made me lose my head" part.

Michelle and Adrianna. Heads turned when we walked the streets arm in arm in imitation of Parisian girls. My bold Neapolitan darkness a foil for your delicate blondness. I was strikingly beautiful when we were together. Miniskirts had just come into style, but not for us. We cared as little for fashion as for politics. You bought a black and white checkered wool coat so bold it suffocated your beauty. It was a coat I could have worn to great effect.

Five centuries before you were born, Fra Filippo Lippi painted your exquisite face over and over again. I startled at the first sight of the likeness—a *Madonna* in the Uffizi. It was on a trip to Florence with my parents, part of their European tour.

The Madonna leans lightly on the edge of a deep frame Lippi painted into the picture. Her head in profile, bent in prayer, casts a shadow upon the frame. A determined Christ child rests a fat little hand on her shoulder. This most secular, earthy of all Florentine religious paintings is said to be a portrait of Lucrezia Buti, the nun with whom Lippi, an unwilling Carmelite monk, had a passionate affair. An angel in the foreground angles half out of the frame, his clump of a wing unconvincing, looks back at the painter, grinning. He may well be a portrait of their son.

Michelle means "gift from God." "Close to God" in Hebrew. You were like an angel descended unto earth, haloed by golden curls. A living cliché.

My name, Adrianna, means "of the Adriatic," hence dark, black.

I bought the Lippi catalogue, a poster of the *Madonna and Child and two Angels*, and a postcard of it too. I kept them in my suitcase when I came back to Paris, hidden from you. I didn't know why. The poster and catalogue didn't survive my relocations, but I still have the postcard. I keep it together with the photograph you rescued our sophomore year.

≈

Back in Paris, under the guidance of Madame Vaudinet, I wrote a paper on Paul Valéry's *La Jeune Parque* (in stumbling French as if Valéry wasn't difficult enough to begin with). You too? I don't remember. Like all our studies that year, this would have been easier for you, fluent in French along with English. Your mother came from Toulouse. Or was it Lausanne? Was she Swiss, not French? How could I not know?

My student essays are lost, but I still have the *Jeune Parque* paperback, my penciled marginalia—mostly in English—faded. Even the exclamation points and asterisks have dimmed. Dimmed along with my memory of what I wrote about the poem, only the passion of it is still vivid, the nights of frenzied writing. I doubt I came to any understanding of Valéry, but I read myself into his young heroine's intense narcissistic introspection as she confronts her own mortality. *My death, secret child already fully formed.*

I now reread *La Jeune Parque* in an edition with the English on facing pages. Aghast! Was I that person back then? Feeling at one with a narrator "who weeps in her own mirror from self-pity." Was I "trapped in the hopeless confines of my thought's inferno." Was I "secretly armed with my inner void . . . my nostril married to the wind from the orange grove"? Oh how on earth did you put up with me! You were not such a narcissist. Easily wounded by the slightest remark, yes, but just as sensitive to the pain of others.

Now, as I finger the pages, my nostrils . . . (Plural—why only one for the *jeune parque*? A detail I never questioned along with so much else.) As I was about to write—my *two* nostrils now breathe in the lingering aroma of the herbs and garlic I chopped for dinner. My grandchildren are coming over for Nonna's special spaghetti. I inhale the here and now and oh god how I wish you were here and now.

You read passages of *La Jeune Parque* aloud to me in perfect, delicate French, less impassioned than my over-the-top recitations. And more heartbreaking. To be fair, the poem reads a lot more convincingly in French. Wonderful, in fact. A plenitude of roiling cadences lost in the English. *La narine jointe au vent de l'oranger* and *de mon néant secrètement armée* still sound magnificent to my ear. And *mes enfers pensifs* when translated literally as "my pensive infernos" (as I probably would have back then) becomes compellingly romantic.

≈

The turmoil of my readings of Racine and Valéry was supplemented by thrashings and wailings of incomprehensible grief and rage piercing through the flimsy new wall that partitioned off our apartment from that of Madame Couteau, our landlady. You were more affected by her suffering than I was. At first I thought the name Couteau a joke. But no, it was her actual name. Madame the Knife on the other side of the wall, behind doors always locked. Her husband had escaped with his life to live in Marseilles, leaving her in the care of Denise who had a room in the garret above us. Denise was tough. She made it clear she didn't like *les jeune filles Americaines*, not even a *bonjour* as she passed by on the stairway, but she tolerated us.

Unlike Madame Couteau. She once escaped as far as our shared foyer as we were leaving. *Juives! Juives sales!* she screamed. We were not Jewish although my dark looks might have suggested I was. Only now do I learn that your Polish father was a closeted Jew, a refugee. Did Madame Couteau know something we didn't? Did you know?

Juives! Juives sales! We knew better than to correct Madame Couteau. Although we did set the record straight for Denise as she led Madame away. Just in case that was why she wouldn't give us the time of day. Not that it changed much.

≈

I read Valéry's *Evening with Monsieur Teste*, which boosted my self-fashioning as an intellectual. Edmond Teste, a man of "incomparable intellectual gymnastics" Valéry wrote, was another paragon of self-absorption. He was, like the *Jeune Parque*, a self portrait of his author. "I endlessly delight in my own brain," Valéry wrote elsewhere. And then I read *A Letter from Madame Émilie Teste*, a loving wife overwhelmed by her husband's extraordinary intellect: *I am a plaything of his muscular thought . . .* A plaything of his muscular thought . . . I related to her too. I yearned for consuming, sacrificial love, yearned to be the woman behind a great man at the same time

I aspired to be a great thinker on my own. Could I be both Edmond and Émilie?

You had no need for such questions. No need for intellectual self-fashioning. Born into a family of professors, writers, and scientists, you had the education and genes my family could not provide me. You were a natural, not pushing for fancy highbrow gymnastics, your thinking purer and more honest than mine, not an act of will. I worked at being smart.

≈

Once at daybreak, after a tumultuous night of reading and writing—you had gone to sleep—I heard some girls, Irish or maybe English—I heard their clear voices outside our windows on the Rue de Seine singing the song of the Dublin fishmonger Sweet Molly Malone.

> *She wheeled her wheelbarrow*
> *Through streets broad and narrow*
> *Crying cockles and mussels,*
> *alive, alive oh ah yea*
> *Alive, alive oh, alive, oh ah yea*

You were curled up in the big bed in the other room on that dawn of cockles and mussels; it was my week for the hard, knobby sofa in the living room. I sang the song of Molly Malone to you the next morning over the *café au lait* and baguette that had become our way, the French way, to start the day. The first verse of that song became another motif of the year. I don't think we knew the final ones in which *her ghost wheels her barrow through streets broad and narrow*, or, if we did, they weren't part of our repertoire. I would belt out my "crying cocks and muscles" version, but not when you were around. You, Filippo Lippi Madonna, would have been offended by such vulgarity. Or so I thought.

≈

Madame Couteau's rantings were especially in keeping with my reading of Céline's *Voyage to the End of the Night,* every page an explosion of rage and insults in a voice the French call his *délire*. Céline had died of a brain aneurysm a few years before our arrival in Paris (though not young and not handsome) but the French students we meet in cafés were all still reading him. Was it Roger or Françoise who first turned me on to Céline? He was not part of our educational program. His writings were, in fact, difficult to reconcile with my enthusiasm for the readings on our curriculum. For one, Céline despised Racine thinking him Jewish—as was the case for everyone he disliked. (Was the same true for Madame Couteau?) If I'd had to choose between the two, Céline would have had my vote. The passion and innovation of his writing are such as to forgive him his nihilism, misogyny, and anti-Semitism. Even Jewish writers found him to be "a great liberator," as Philip Roth did.

You didn't read Céline, but kept to the proscribed classics and Valéry. Was it because, French being your mother tongue, you couldn't stomach Céline's obscenities, his sneering cynicism, his foul-mouthed slang that I couldn't register in my gut. Yet even in the English edition I now read (not the new one reissued to great acclaim) his rants come through with intense physicality. . . . *we are nothing but packages of fetid, half-rotted viscera . . . more unfortunate than shit.*

Yet Céline was not a bad person. *The sadness of the world has different ways of getting to people,* he wrote. He was a doctor like my will-do-in-a-pinch lover Francis, but unlike Francis whose ambition was to end up in a fancy hospital, Céline treated the destitute and marginalized of the poorest Paris suburbs.

Amidst Céline's rabid thrashings against corruption and death (his own and others'), amidst the *Jeune Parque's* agonizing over her own mortality, amidst Valéry's dying Edmond Test, amidst the deaths of Racine's heroes and heroines (poison for Phaedre)—amidst all those confrontations of death, we sang: *Michelle my belle . . . Y a Mustapha . . . Alive, alive oh, alive, oh ah yea . . .*

We were alive, oh ah yea. Day and night. Mme. Couteau cried out, stomped, and pounded the walls. Denise clacked up and down the broad stone stairs of our *immeuble* and late at night there were heavier footsteps followed by the back-and-forth creaking of her bedsprings. Alive, alive oh, alive, oh ah yea.

≈

Blaise, Francis, and Professeur Lavoie's penetrating kisses had receded into the past by mid-ocean in the exuberant craziness of our Atlantic crossing on a student ship. It was there I met Alex, the dramatic Greek dramaturge I would marry way too young. Racine's Phaedra, her impulses gone wild, Valéry's narcissists, Émilie Teste's subjugation to her brilliant husband, and Céline's extravagant nihilism were still coursing through my brain, a heady mix that ripened me for the picking.

≈

There was no email, no Facebook to keep us connected during my nine years in Greece. Yes, we did write occasional letters, fewer and fewer as we were caught up in our separate lives. I didn't tell you when I had a backroom abortion. Or about the stray dog I rescued right afterwards or when, years later, the dog died. Those years are not part of this reminiscence except as a reason—the reason—I was far, oh so far from you. Paris, French writers, pop songs, and desperate, misguided attempts at love are what this story is about.

When I saw you next it had been a year since we'd written. I was moving to California where my husband had a new job, but I planned a stopover on the East Coast, primarily to see you, the one friend with whom I had kept in touch.

It was only when I called to arrange a time to meet that you told me you had a child. His name is Adrian, you said in the same matter-of-fact tone as when, eleven years before, you told me you were no longer a virgin. I could only presume he was my namesake. I didn't ask. Too much time had gone by. I wanted to say I was big bellied and would soon have a baby too, but the words wouldn't come.

≈

It was early summer and you were at a house by the sea in Rhode Island. As I drove up a sandy driveway you came into view. You were sitting on a white wicker love seat leaning towards your baby propped on blue cushions beside you. All the sparkle of the ocean, all the glory of the masses of day lilies fronting the porch, all the sunshine of that clear summer day, all were incarnate in that scene.

The moment I learned you had a baby I envisioned you and your infant as Filippo Lippi's Madonna. The New England seaside setting was a contrast to Lippi's background of somber fields and craggy mountain peaks, a difference I hadn't considered but hardly noticed.

It was the sight of the child that took me aback as I got out of the car and walked towards the porch. Yes, he had your blue eyes, Michelle, but his hair was as dark as mine and his skin dusky olive, like mine. It was as if you had birthed my baby. You hadn't mentioned the father.

When I turned to look at you, I was taken aback a second time. Your beautiful hair slashed short flared jaggedly around a face bloated and coarsened almost beyond recognition. I searched for the delicate Lippi Madonna buried there. It had to be there.

I ran up the steps of the porch and wedged my protruding belly close to you, hugging and kissing and reaching towards Adrian. I felt your body stiffen. I'd forgotten you didn't know I was pregnant. That you too would be struck by the unexpected. I backed away to a nearby chair and waited for you to speak.

You mentioned the nice weather.

Adrian is incredibly beautiful, I said. What a precious gift, I added, immediately ashamed of the cliché.

He's the product of a one-night stand. The father was passing through town and I never saw him again.

A one-night stand? Doesn't seem like you. More like something I might do. Did do, in fact—more than once, I added with a shrug. I wanted you to feel ok about yourself.

Doesn't seem like me! Not the perfect, do-no-wrong Michelle you expected. How could you assume I'd be the same person you thought I was? And look at you. Married nine years and having a baby. You, wild girl, always in heat, chasing after one man or another, reciting reams of poetry you didn't understand. You were horrid, obnoxious—and totally amazing. All these years I hoped the crazy Adrianna I loved would come back to me. But no! Here's the good little wife padding after her husband wherever he goes. And pregnant too!

I reached for you. You stood up. So did I.

I've missed you, Michelle. So very, very much. I'm not that different. And who are you to get upset about my being pregnant. You have a baby!

But not a husband. You still don't get it, do you?

You turned away towards a table beside the loveseat. Would you like some ice tea? The coldness of your tone echoed the clink of cubes poured from the frosted pitcher.

Desperate to retrieve the Michelle of the Paris year, I began to whisper our old song: *Michelle ma belle, Michelle, ma belle. Sont des mots* . . .

Your pained look silenced me. I put down the glass you handed me and leaned over to pick up Adrian. You blocked my way. Seated again, I gulped down my tea trying not to cry. I'm so sorry, so sorry. Please, I'm so very, very sorry. You gripped your baby so tightly in your arms that he began to cry. I got up and ran towards the car leaving behind, still unwrapped, the plush teddy bear wearing the "I love Paris" t-shirt I'd bought for the baby.

Where had you gone my beloved Filippo Lippi Michelle? Where were you? Who was this angry person lashing out at me?

I was flying to California the next day. There was no time for a second visit. Would it have made a difference?

≈

You wrote only once more, shortly after I arrived in California. A brief note, polite, thanking me for the gift and for stopping by. My son was born. He never slept more than three hours at a stretch. My husband left me for a California girl. I was dangerously emaciated from fatigue and grief. I wrote my misery to you, my only friend in the world. You didn't answer.

Worried I'd burdened you with my troubles, I sent a second letter saying I was fine, my husband was back in full loving remorse, my baby sleeping most nights. The only time I lied to you. I tried to call. Your phone had been disconnected.

Weeks later came a letter from your brother. You and your baby were dead. Suicide. Your lives ended not long after our meeting on the white porch of sunshine and daylilies. No word as to how or why or where. I—sleep-deprived single mother in a swamp of soggy diapers, nipples raw and leaking, translating for a living with my baby bound to my chest in a snuggly as I worked—I never asked. Your death localized only in a remote area of my brain.

It was months later, looking down at my sleeping child, that the shock of what you had done hit me. How anyone could kill their baby?

As I sit writing of what happened so long ago, the harsh sound of a saw cutting through wood jags through my windows from the park across the street. A limb severed? Or the tree itself felled? For the first time in all these years I wonder how you ended your lives. Were they literally cut short? A slice of a blade? Madame Couteau a presage?

Or did you, so afraid of heights, leap from a high window, your baby in your arms?

Was it a pharmaceutical death? Like poison as for Phaedre.

Did you cradle your son as the Madonna cradles an infant Jesus across her lap in paintings that anticipate his deposition from the Cross? *Pietà*. Filippo Lippi never painted such a *Pietà*. I could have told you that.

Pietà. Is it the thought of the child that still pains me the most? Is it only as a mother that I can mourn your death, the child more real to me than you ever were? Were you no more than a painting, your face in profile, just as in my memory of you framed in a doorway holding a discarded photograph? Were you no more than a Beatles song? Or was it that I needed to see you as a Madonna, holy and pure, needed that image to overlay the livingness of you? Needed the distance of a painting and a song, the who of you disturbing in ways I didn't understand? Didn't want to understand? Needed not to know who you were?

The rescued photograph is faded to a dull brown, the halo of golden curls dimmed, but your eyes still squint against the light of that long ago sun. You are looking straight at me, the hint of a smile curving your lips, as I take the photograph. Behind the camera, one eye peering into the viewfinder, I saw only a face to be contained within the margins of a picture.

≈

The tomato I slice for lunch spills its innards onto the wood cutting board. The tenderly washed lettuce leaves are torn apart. A loud groan reverberates from the park. The entire tree smashes to the ground.

OLÉ

I was woken at dawn by my grandmother's screams.

"My God! The roses! Oh my God, the roses. Charles! Oh, Charles, be careful! Oh the roses!"

She was leaning out the second-story bedroom window overlooking her garden. Below my grandfather waved his arms frantically at Olé the bull, loose again, wreaking havoc on the lawn and heading straight for the luscious, overblown, pink blossoms that my grandmother tended with a fanaticism that bordered on lunacy.

My grandfather's long white nightshirt flapped like loose sheets of paper, accented by the bobbing pompom of his nightcap as he zigzagged in front of the bull, trying to head him off.

"Git! Git! Git!"

Olé advanced, bellowing.

"Charles! My God, Charles," screamed my grandmother from above.

Olé came to an abrupt halt a foot away from my grandfather, lowering his massive head and pawing the ground with one hoof.

"Git! Git! Git!" yelled my grandfather, standing firm in front of the roses. Framed by blossoms, his arms in their full white sleeves waving up and down, he looked like a demented guardian angel.

Olé snorted, turned, and ambled slowly towards the barn. My grandfather walked behind him, his arms now by his side, the fabric of his garment settled into long peaceful folds, the morning ritual ended.

GLORIA

1. BED

Four-poster Queen. Bought after Daniel and the dog died. First Daniel, then Harpo. The King, lumped by their tossings and slumbers, become an intolerable expanse. Gloria considered a replacement Full, but too much of a comedown. Besides, you never knew. She was only eighty-one when Daniel died. Now that she's ninety-one a Full would do. Although she still keeps an eye out, notices the presence or absence of a wedding ring. Not that absence equals availability. Recently she checked out an Old Geezer waiting for the bus in front of her high-rise. No ring. New to the neighborhood. Or maybe just visiting? Probably just visiting. Old Geezers don't move except to nursing homes. She'd guessed he was about ten years younger than she.

She lies on her side, hugging an oversize pillow under her arm to keep her gimpy shoulder from collapsing inward. "Spooning," said Gilda, her physical therapist. Medicare gives Gloria seventeen PT visits a year. Seventeen golden Gildas. Gilda would like Gloria to sleep on her back. "Much better for your spine." Gloria has tried, with only rampant insomnia to show for her efforts. She imagines Japanese sleeping on tatami beds, bricks under their heads. Gilda's not asking her to go Japanese. "If you must sleep on your side…" Gilda tries hard not to be judgmental or disapproving, but every now and then

Gloria detects a tangy underscent in the sweetness that is Gilda. Bitter lemon beneath the primary infusion of blackberry musk. "If you *must*," the stress ever so gentle, "*must* sleep on your side, put a pillow under your armpit, like spooning." "Spooning?" "Yes. Cuddling, snuggling, like when a guy curls up behind you in bed, wraps himself around you." "Oh my, that's been a while." "For me too," Gilda says.

At therapy last week Walter was dropping a pencil onto the industrial carpeting and creaking over slowly to pick it up, gripping onto the arm of a chair for support. "Look Gilda! Look!" Gilda was distracted helping another client cope with the disabilities of the ancient. Walter's plump wife Rachel took up the slack. "That's great Walter! All that hard work pays off." He was beaming. They must still be spooning. Picking up a pencil may be a major accomplishment for Walter, but he doesn't hug a pillow every night to ward off pain and sorrow.

≈

Shoulders. Arm. Pain. Everyone has a different explanation. Sara, the masseuse she saw before starting therapy, thought it was simply a matter of tight muscles. "Well, if you really want to have arthritis . . ." she said when Gloria brought up the possibility. The other Sarah, the Sarah with an "h," the personal trainer her daughter Zoe had hired, said it was all because of Gloria's bad posture. "Whole left side fucked up," she claimed. Only she didn't say "fucked up." That's Gloria's translation of Sarah's "out of alignment." Everything that's wrong with

Gloria's body is on the left. Left foot that had to be operated, back pain on the left, damaged left kidney. Analytical side of the brain. At least her creative right is more or less intact.

A part of her likes her infirmities, the attention they garner. If only they didn't hurt. Physical therapy is the best, even when it hurts. It's the only carnal contact she gets, apart from her daughters' hugs. Sabrina is more attentive than her sister, but her hugs are quick and perfunctory. Hi-Mom, bye-Mom hugs. Zoe, always the more dramatic, gives her long, tight squeezes with loud, smacking kisses on both cheeks. My God, where would she be without them? Gloria feels a sudden rush of love, a rush as deep and intense as her first out-of-belly holding of their puckered little bodies.

Daniel's shoulders were hunched, even as a young man, perhaps as a boy. Same for his brother. Teenagers walking around with the posture of old bookkeepers. At first Gloria thought scoliosis, but no, there was no curvature of the spine. His stoop irritated her when they began dating. Gradually it became acceptable, almost unnoticeable, and then endearing. She'd see him walking along, shoulders permanently rounded, neck scrunched up so his head could face directly forward, crown of curly hair parallel to the ground, and think, how sweet. Her heart would skip the proverbial beat. She'd tried to straighten him once, at the beginning, put her hands on his shoulders and pressed backwards, only to find a firm settlement of resistance. "Doesn't it hurt to walk that way?" she'd asked. "Not in the least." He'd been mildly surprised by the question, tolerating her efforts at his self-improvement with gently dismissive humor, as he would tolerate the antics of a puppy nipping at his heels. Learning to let him stoop was one of the great lessons of her life.

Old Geezer's shoulders were hunched. She wonders if they'd always been so.

Gloria rolls over to the getting-up side, the side nearest the door. Daniel's side. She commandeered it after he died. Let's not get analytical. Quicker route to the bathroom is more like it. Harpo still alive and sharing the bed, but he didn't object. He always had the middle. Most of their dogs had the middle. Living contraceptives. Daniel's joke.

Getting out of the high four-poster has become a challenge, one she keeps a secret. Ten years ago she would stretch the length of her body while still supine, delighting in the coming-to-action of rested muscle and sinew. Now she rolls carefully to one side, attentive not to press too hard on the gimpy shoulder. She swings her legs sideways. They dangle almost to the floor. They used to reach the floor. Or did they? Getting out of bed was one sweeping motion, automatic, thoughtless. She pushes her torso to verticality, stretches her left arm out onto the bedside table for balance and stands. A deep breath and she totters off to the bathroom.

2. RUG

She's careful not to trip on the hall rug, a hand-knotted Tabriz, deep mustard yellows and wine reds threadbare softened. She and Daniel bought it at a yard sale upstate New York on one of their weekends in the country. Her daughters want it removed, want all rugs removed. "Wall to wall would be so much easier. Cut down on noise too." Noise? Age takes care of that. Gloria hasn't acquired a hearing aid, but it's on her agenda.

At what point did the act of walking require all her concentration? She prefers to think of it as mindfulness, Buddhist mindfulness. Mindful walking. Do all arthritis-riddled aged become Buddhist by necessity? Being in the moment a matter of survival? Distraction a luxury? Inattention fatal? Spirituality by fiat. It's the closest she's come to religion despite almost being born in the cathedral of St. John the Divine during Christmas service, the only time the family went to church. Her mother was singing at top voice Glo . . .oh. . .oh. . .oh. . .oh. . .oh! when contractions accelerated. She rushed off to the hospital mid-excelsis, before Deo.

Imposed mindfulness is not all bad. Gloria has rushed through life. Deep breathing left her impatient. Breathe in: LET. Breathe out: GO. L E T G O. A mantra that April, a neurotic, angry Yoga teacher once taught her. Living example of its inefficacy. Her cheery name didn't do her much good either.

Even now Gloria reads too fast, just as she used to make love too fast, wanting to get to the end, worried everything wouldn't turn out right. Maybe no orgasm, maybe the beloved protagonist dies, dies young, dies horribly, a suicide maybe, or fatal accident just as she or he has finally found happiness. Happened to someone whom someone she knows knew. Fell in love with a wonderful woman and was hit by a truck. "Never have I been so happy," he'd said. "Never did I think it possible to be so happy." Well, guess what? It wasn't possible. Kaboom. Life over in an instant. Would he have had time to think in that instant? Realize such happiness is not possible? His thought? Singular thought. No time for plurals. No plurals when you're hit by a truck. Kaboom. Over. Nada. LET GO. No choice there.

She hopes Old Geezer won't be hit by a truck.

Mostly she makes it on time to the bathroom in the morning, but yesterday she didn't and had quite a dribble to clean up. She doesn't want Nella, the big Irishwoman who comes to help out, to be aware of her little accidents. Nella would tell the children and then it would be the old folks' home. The cleanup took some time. All the bending and swabbing and drying. Everything takes time. "Aren't you bored Mom?" her daughters ask. "What do you do all day?" "Oh, I keep busy enough with this and that," Gloria replies. Survival, that's what she does all day, survive. It takes up a lot of time when you're ninety-one.

3. SASH

Bladder emptied, she traverses the Tabriz rug again. Safely back in the bedroom, she eases into her bathrobe, gimpy left arm first. Ties the sash. Arthritic fingers still do the job. The sash is patterned with hearts. White, yellow, and pink outlines of hearts. Other hearts filled in: blue, pink, red, and green. Small hearts, all the same size, an inch at their widest, scattered topsy turvy up, down, sideways against a dull gray background. The background a shade darker than the gray of the bathrobe, a long-ago thrift shop find that was missing its sash. Gloria filched the strip of sprinkled hearts from another thrift shop item, a wraparound she gave Nella. No one would notice the mismatch. Anyway, who sees her in her bathrobe? Not even Nella. Gloria makes a point of being dressed when Nella arrives at 10:00. Not because of the sash from the deprived wraparound she gave her. No. Because Gloria knows that Nella, hired by her daughters, is there to spy on her. She comes for two hours every other day, excessive for cleaning, but not for spying. Gloria is always vigilant, on guard. She will not be put in an old folks' home.

She wishes someone were there in the morning to see her in her bathrobe. A comfortable man enjoying the frowziness together. A man to go with the hearts that hold the soft, fuzzy robe around her, a man to keep her warm. Daniel would not have noticed the mismatched sash or the sprinkled hearts. Noticing was not the point.

4. CURTAINS

Gloria draws open the heavy, off-white, Home Depot window curtains on the other side of the bed, her getting-up side before Daniel died. She has an intimate view of the new couple in the apartment on the fourteenth floor of the annex across the airshaft. She's on fifteen. They have no curtains. A row of rooms— bathroom, bedroom, living room, kitchen—all with big windows opening onto the airshaft and not a single shade or curtain. Gloria figured it was because they hadn't gotten around to putting them up, but it's been a month now. They seem oblivious to being on display. They're in the bathroom, as usual this time of morning, the same time Gloria draws open her curtains. The woman, hugely pregnant, smoothes oil over her extended belly, the man rubs deodorant onto his raised armpits. Not acts of exhibitionism. Clean-cut Americans they are. Her bouncy ponytail, his crew cut. Energetic movements. Even pregnant, she doesn't waddle. Gloria has named them Sally and Nick.

When she and Daniel lived on 20th Street, a gay couple directly across the street from their eleventh floor apartment danced nude in the evening under bright overhead lights. Not cheek to cheek dancing—Gloria knows the double entendre— but great leaps and twirls, balls and dicks jiggling and flapping. That was exhibitionism! No underarm deodorant applications involved. Gloria thought of asking the men to put up curtains. Sabrina and Zoe were six and four. But she reminded herself that she was an open-minded, progressive mother who wasn't going to have her children grow up thinking nudity was a bad thing. When Gloria went back to teaching middle school, once the girls were full-time in school, she made sure her science courses included Comprehensive Sexuality Education.

Sally and Nick are getting dressed. The day has begun. The building staff is below, hauling garbage. The men yell in Spanish. Gloria is taking Spanish classes once a week at the Jewish Senior Center. She's not Jewish and the instructor is not Spanish, but the center is only three blocks away. She gets there on her own, despite the protests of Sabrina and Zoe. Learning Spanish is better for lubricating rusty mental cogs than the proscribed crossword puzzles, which have no other use, as far as Gloria can see. With Spanish, she will understand what they're shouting at the bottom of the airshaft.

5. TV

In the kitchen she turns on the TV. A small, old TV, screen lightly convex. Its mechanism protrudes back over the counter, occupying prime kitchen real estate. It was always the radio in the morning when Daniel was alive. Switched on the moment one or the other entered the kitchen. After he died, Gloria began turning on the TV for breakfast, the one the two of them had watched only when they ate dinner in the kitchen. Not a deliberate decision. Just what she did. She doesn't like the anchor on the MSNBC seven o'clock news, but there's comfort in his bullish body and the hyped-up talk mingling with the robust aroma of coffee and crisp toast, and the faint, softly bitter scent emanating from the jar of multi-vitamins.

Sally and Nick watch a lot of TV. On a big flat screen about the size of their living room window. Gloria can see the picture as clearly as if it were in her apartment. More clearly than she can see Sally and Nick. They're smaller and not digitalized. No sound in either case. Perhaps in summer. She hopes not. This morning in the kitchen he's talking, gesticulating forcefully. He's standing. She's sitting, looking up at him through her wire-frame glasses, ponytail bobbing. She hopes they aren't having a quarrel. He's pulling a flat pan of something brown and crusty out of the oven. Seems he's the one who does the cooking.

Old Geezer shuffles into Sally and Nick's kitchen. So that's where he's visiting! Or perhaps he's come to stay.

6. COFFEE

She's had to give up caffeinated coffee, but she allows herself a cup of decaf in the morning. So what if she drops dead a few months early. A brain scan showed three mini strokes. Three black spots, pinpoint size. She wouldn't have seen them had the doctor not pointed them out. She wasn't aware of having had strokes. She went for the MRI because she was afraid of losing her mind like her mother. Medicare paid. She didn't tell Sabrina and Zoe. Normal for your age, the neurologist said. At 91 she doesn't want to be normal for her age.

Sabrina would have her drinking only herbal tea. She gives Gloria loose tea. She's against tea bags. The ecology. "Such a waste, Mom." Whatever. Gloria puts the tea in the little round strainer, also courtesy of Sabrina. She screws it tight, but leaves still escape. Her tea always has bits of stuff floating on the surface. Yesterday it was RISHI ORGANIC SERENE. Golden colored infusion with lofty notes of citrus blossoms and lavender. Caffeine-Free. Just greenery. Organic. Serene. Can't do any harm. She misses her strong afternoon cups of Lipton with heaping scoops of white sugar.

Her decaf is in the yellow cup with purple squiggles that she bought years ago at the Salvation Army. It sits on a round heater she ordered from a catalogue. She orders a lot from catalogues. Lillian Vernon, Signatures, Handsome Rewards … Gloria cups her hand over the red button on the heater to see if it's lit. She's forgetful about things. Has to check everything at least twice.

Gloria loves Jello. The texture. Slides down cool and easy. Lemon's her favorite. She makes a bowl about every other day. Sabrina tells her to make it from scratch. "Buy gelatin and mix it with juice. Easy Mom. Better for you. Less sugar and no fake colors." Sabrina reads labels. Especially food labels. She takes forever to buy groceries, what with reading all the fine print. Dave won't go grocery shopping with her anymore. I'll meet you in an hour to help with the bags, he'll say. He's a good husband. Just doesn't want to stand around reading fine print on cans and cartons. Don't blame him. Gloria buys what Sabrina tells her isn't poison, but sometimes she buys things that are poison. When she can't get out of bed anymore she'll buy only poison. Cheese Doodles, Fritos, Hostess Twinkies, Oreo cookies, Strawberry Pop Tarts. She'll die happy.

She'll bring Sally and Nick a pot of chicken paprikash, Sabrina and Zoe's favorite dish. They've banned cream from their diets, but now and then it's "Mom, make chicken paprikash." Ultimate comfort food. A culinary hug. She hopes Old Geezer likes chicken paprikash.

7. CHAIR

Back in the bedroom she notices a new chair in Sally and Nick's bedroom. Maybe not new, but a chair moved within Gloria's cut-off view of the room. A large, plushy, brown rocking chair at the foot of the bed. A chair to nurse the baby in the middle of the night. So they're not going to take the baby to bed to nurse. Responsible parents. That's good.

Gloria imagines sitting in the chair with the baby in her arms. Or on the new white sofa in their living room. (They'll soon learn the folly of a white sofa!) When the baby's born, she plans to ring the doorbell and offer to help. She can't be trusted to walk with an infant. Yet sitting holding the baby would be helpful. Coos and grunts as she cradles the chubby little girl in her arms. Gassy smile. Sweet smell of baby piss. Even shit smells sweet when you love a baby. Gloria used to lift her babies up high to smell their diapered derrieres. Time for a change? Seems so. She never knew how much she could love before her babies came. She would have died for them without a second's hesitation. Would she die for them now? Sure, she's old, going to die soon anyway, but it's not the same. When had she stopped being certain she would unthinkingly throw herself under a car to save their lives? At what point did the moment of hesitation come into play? Their high school? College? Marriage? When did self-preservation trump survival of the species?

Do Sally and Nick know if it's going to be a boy or a girl? Would Gloria have wanted to know the sex of her unborn babies? She was certain she was having girls despite everyone's saying they were going to be boys because she carried way out front. Sally is carrying way out front. It's probably a boy. Gloria would prefer a girl. She's glad she had girls.

The other day she met Rudy, her downstairs neighbor Lucy's boy. Lucy had just bought the Poang chair that the girls gave Gloria for her last birthday. A reading chair that turned out horridly uncomfortable. Lucy called Rudy to carry it downstairs, but he didn't answer the phone so the two of them went to get him. Gloria didn't need to go along, she just likes to see people's homes, likes to see how they live. You can tell a lot from things, what they are and how they're arranged.

Gloria didn't exactly meet Rudy. The big lump of a teenager was asleep on the sofa in front of a darkened laptop. The entire half hour of her visit the boy never stirred. Playing possum? Can't blame him. Why should a teenager meet an old woman? If he pretended, he did a good job of it. Gloria watched to catch a flicker of movement. Nada.

"Like a bump on a log," Gloria's mother used to say. "Don't sit there like a bump on a log." Gloria pays attention to bumps on logs on her daily walks in the park across the street. Gray, brown, pink, orange swells of mushrooms, some small as pinheads, others big as upside-down teacups. Bumps of bark, protective scabs where a tree has suffered injury. Moving pro-trusions—scurrying insects, slithering worms. Metamorphoses. Emanations from within, attachments from without. Daphne emerging from a tree trunk in the statue by Bernini. Ovid in rewind. A bump on a log is not a bad thing. Gloria will think of the boy downstairs as a bump on a log awaiting metamorphosis.

≈

A colorful contraption has appeared in Sally and Nick's living room. A baby bouncer. Plunk in baby and any movement sets the tiny tot bobbing and jiggling. "Delightful stationary entertainer with an array of fun toys and activities for little explorers." Gloria knows the spin because Sabrina bought one when Ellen was born. Gloria never had such things for her girls and they grew up just fine.

8. ELEVATOR

The other day Gloria met them in the elevator. Going down. A sudden stop on the next floor and there they were, fully clothed.

Sally's face was not as Gloria'd expected. She'd imagined a pert round face with a rosebud mouth to match the merry swish of her blond ponytail. She was unprepared for the strong jaw line, broad forehead, big-toothed grin.

"Rachel," Sally said, extending a hand. "My husband Ezra." Gloria hadn't thought Jewish either.

"Gloria," she said, and offered to help should there be an emergency.

"That's huge," Rachel responded. Not something Sally would have said.

Old Geezer was not with them. Gloria was relieved, and surprised to be relieved.

9. BATH

She loves her morning bath. Perfumed, oiled, bubbled, Epsom salted, straight up. Most of her life she took showers. No time for baths. She eases herself cautiously into the tub of hot water, its surface shimmering and slick from the J & J baby oil she's poured into it. She's thankful she can still manage this alone. She can't if she's fearful. Fear is fatal, hesitation lethal. She's had special handles installed to grip as she gets in and out, along with rubber daisies glued to the bottom of the tub. It was Zoe who insisted on the daisies. "Mom, otherwise I'm taking out the whole damn tub." Gloria doesn't like the daisies, thinks they're unsanitary, hard for Nella to clean. Nella loves to clean bathrooms. One day Gloria caught her scraping between the tiles with a wooden toothpick. "Not necessary," she'd admonished.

"Germs, Mrs. Carter, germs. You can't be too careful!"

Sabrina and Zoe would have a fit if they found out about the baby oil. As it is they don't approve of Gloria taking baths. "Mom, it's way too dangerous. What if you fall? It could be a whole day before someone realizes what's happened." Fat chance. Sabrina calls promptly at 8:30 every morning, on her cell phone on the way to work. Zoe does the evening shift, usually at seven, just at the beginning of Gloria's HBO program. Then there's Nella who comes every other day from ten to noon. Gloria figures that on Nella's alternate days if she fell in the bath promptly after Sabrina's call she could go for ten and a half hours before anyone noticed. No use thinking about it. She's not going to be found naked and helpless in the tub or on the bathroom floor. She won't fall. She's not stupid.

She may well drown in the bathtub, but it won't be by accident. Her suicide of choice. Got the idea from her friend Nancy. Second try for Nancy. The first, pills and plastic bag, but the pills were too few and the plastic bag too loose. Second try, pills and whisky and a full tub of hot water into which she slowly and fatally slid.

Gloria has been stockpiling pills for several years. Ambien, Percodan, Oxycodone, Hydrocodon, Trazodone, Tylenol P.M. Anything to dull consciousness. She hides them in the cups of bras she never wears. Sabrina and Zoe know she never wears bras so they won't be tempted to dig them out should it be necessary, God forbid, to dress her.

It's been a long time since she wore a bra. Her breasts are small, one smaller than the other because of a biopsy thirty years ago. The thing was benign. Daniel liked her without a bra. Almost to the day he died, he'd come up behind her and slide his hands under her clothes to cup her breasts. One more thing she misses. She imagines Old Geezer cupping her breasts with his bony hands. It's not a pretty picture.

Gloria will have sunk beneath the waters—pearls that were her eyes—long before her daughters have to dress her. A bubble bath? Perfumed? Lovely. But not yet, definitely not yet. Last year, when they discovered a "thing" on her left lung, she realized how much she wanted to live. The "thing," innocuous, collaborated.

What to wear? She will not be naked. Gross, as her daughters used to say. Usually while looking down at their food. Fussy eaters. Sabrina more than Zoe. "Just one bite. Or no dessert." Gloria misses those days.

A flowing white nightgown. Ophelia style. No flowers though. Wet, the nightgown would cling, but it might balloon up. She'll experiment. Lucky she never got fat. She's been careful about that, although when she lies in the tub her belly rounds gently up to the surface of the water. A hillock where there used to be a gentle valley. Pubic hair, thick black bush, gone. Lucky she still had a bit left before Daniel died.

She will time it so Nella, not one of her daughters, finds her.

Hoarding pills saves Gloria from Substance Abuse. She'd grown especially fond of Oxycodone during the last flare up of arthritis. Slow seep of soft surrender. Languid letting go. She'd stay awake as long as possible. Prolong the pleasure. Savor the drift towards sleep. Deep sleep.

"How old are you?" the doctor had asked. Young doctor. Barely out of high school.

"Well then, take as many as you want." He didn't say, "as many as you need." "As many as you want." Maybe there's truth in right-wing talk of death panels. Kill off the old biddies.

Substance abuse. Substance. Substantial. She has a substantial income. She's a woman of substance. She does not abuse substance. "Take as many as you want." Who does he think she is?

10. PHILODENDRON

The leaves on the hanging philodendron in Sally and Nick's bedroom droop wrinkled and brown from neglect. How is it possible to kill a philodendron? Their only plant. The stuffed rocking chair at the end of the bed has been moved, if not discarded. The baby bouncer in the living room is gone.

Was the baby stillborn? Not even a squinting glimpse of the delivery room? Or had she lived a moment under the bright lights. Her life a moment of fluorescent consciousness.

Daniel died an old man in his sleep. An afternoon nap, Gloria in the next room. "A good death," people said. Gloria wishes she had been curved beside him, spooning.

Old Geezer is gone. Just as well, she thinks.

Turning away from the window, Gloria walks around her bed, through to the hallway where she treads mindfully over the worn Tabriz, noting the felt padding peeking out from under its fringes.

BREATHING

Silvery lines insist oxygen into her nostrils. Breathing is hard. Not like when she used to run, run fast and faster, head of the pack, win, win, win, first to cross the finish line. Back then, chest stretched taut to bursting, gasping for air, she wanted it wanted it wanted it. And back home panting for air his big belly heaving onto her, sweat and slither pant, gasp and grasp, wanting wanting. Precious bitch my love he'd grunt as he rolled to her side and lay like a beached whale breathing hard. Love. Precious bitch. Love. Love. Wanting it. Wanting it.

Breathing was hard after he left. One hand on chest, the other on belly. Equalizing the in and the out, smoothing away jagged gulps of air. Breath in. Breath out. Let. Go. A mantra from a yoga teacher. Let. Go.

Running, sex, yoga long time past. Let. Go. New definition according to a body immobilized in a cranked-up hospital bed, breathing insisted into her lungs. Let Go the labored flow of in and out. Whoosh.

Her doctor tells her that when a patient is breathing his or her last, he switches off the monitor screen. Families and loved ones fixate on it, not on the dying, he explains. True for her. As her mother died, she stared at jagged multicolored lines on a machine and at numbers on a green square on the upper right. She watched her mother die in decreasing numbers and lines scurrying across a black screen.

Let Go. She wants to see her letting go, see the pixilated signs of her own last breaths. She looks up at the electronic tracks of her pulmonary output. Let go, she murmurs. Let Go. The lines zigzag, jagged Everests and Grand Canyons vanishing stage left. Numbers in green go down, down. Alarms screech and beep, beep, LOUD. LOUD. Let go. let go. Let go before nurses come racing in, breathing hard.

ULTIMATUM

Her babies, now in their fifties, have issued an ultimatum: live-in aide or retirement home. The two of them sat right there on her new sofa, looked her in the eye. Your choice, Mom.

Nancy, the younger—always the bossier—had already placed her on a waiting list at Brookhaven not far from where she lives a suburban Connecticut life with husband and two children. You should move before next winter sets in, she said. Think of us. Michael and I worry ourselves sick about you.

Ultimatum. *Ultimare.* Come to an end. *Ultimata.* Ultimatums. The words roll gently on the tongue, belie the harshness of their meaning. Winter. Ice. ICE. Ultimatums.

TRIPLING OF ICE FORCE   DEPORTATIONS TO BEGIN

Winters in her Manhattan apartment come to an end? Yes, she's mostly housebound when walking is perilous, but there's take-out: Vietnamese, Thai, Japanese, Chinese, Indian, even hamburgers and fries. She's happy nesting in the big chair by the window watching cars inch by and buses lumber to a soft stop disgorging intrepid passengers into a whitened morning. And the dogs! The dogs in the park across the street leap and run in a frenzy of delight—big dogs jump over little ones jacketed in plaids. Many live in her building and she gets her fill of waggles and licks in the elevator and lobby. It's been years since her rescue dog, Carlos, died, yet she's still part of the scene, even if not vigorously so.

Vigorous, vigor. Not a common word these days. She looked it up on line. As a teacher of English as a second language, the communality of words was important to check or she'd risk introducing obscure words from her extensive vocabulary. Looking up the diminishment of a word's recurrence became an addiction, especially after retirement.

Vigor: the lines on a chart peak in the 1850s and stumble downhill from then to the present. The word also loses its vigor.

Not that Betty doesn't get out. Not a quitter. "Give in but don't give up," is a recent motto. *I am a hearth of spiders these days: a nest of trying* (Ada Limón).

She's not sure what to make of the spiders yet the image makes sense. She is a nest of trying. Trying not to get lost, not to be caught in the wide web of her wandering mind. She makes notes, schedules, accommodates, adjusts to what is possible.

She rides buses these days. She can manage subway stairs, just not the push and shove of passengers. And the pole dancers! She once cheered them on, celebrated their spinning twists to muscular horizontals, their flips to prance on the ceiling. Then, as she aged she could see all that could go wrong. In what had seemed joyful she saw only danger. She'd hold her breath, anxiety mounting, as when she saw her youngest grandchildren scramble and swing on jungle gyms.

Yes, she could distance herself from the subway acrobats, take a far seat. It was the shuffling supplicants supplicating the length of the cars she couldn't avoid. *Ladies and*

Gentlemen... don't want to disturb ... need something to eat... please help... just got out of hospital ... God bless. A lot is scam, money goes to drugs, still that's not what gets to her. Scam or not, it's desperation. Like so much that is desperation in these desperate times. The pole dancers seem desperate too.

ROHINGYA REFUGEES LIVING IN LARGEST REFUGEE CAMP IN THE WORLD

Betty volunteered at a homeless shelter in the Bronx for twenty years until getting there became too difficult and, yes, frightening. She'd get confused, disoriented by demolitions and constructions that blocked sidewalks forcing her to cross the street and upending her sense of direction.

Some of the women still keep in touch. Donna, whose speech was so mumbled as to be almost incomprehensible (years of blow jobs, she explained), tells Betty she's been hired as a receptionist in a doctor's office. Over the phone, Donna's vowels and consonants are carefully articulated—the result of the hours, weeks, months they'd spent transforming slurred utterances into crisp pronouncements. Not exactly ESL, but Betty's years of teaching were put to use.

Haydee also calls. Haydee, who insisted on doing Betty's nails, five months pregnant when she lost the baby, now has a job in a nail salon.

Oh, Betty misses them, but she's resigned to signing petitions on the web and donating to worthy causes: Mercy Corps, Fresh Air Fund, Amnesty, ACLU, and the like. Black Lives

Matter too. White Guilt. Privileged Guilt. Survivor's Guilt as the planet erupts, floods, burns, melts, as bees and butterflies and owls die out. Species lost forever.

And intimate, domestic guilts. Not paying greater attention to the children, not remembering a friend's birthday. The shameful extra glass of wine. Skipping chair yoga class, skipping flossing at night. Guilt for feeling guilty. Moral defect? Loosen up, she tells herself. There's only so much you can do.

Ultimatum. *Ultimata*. Ultimatums. She's besieged by *ultimata*.

DEPORTATIONS TO BEGIN

DREAMERS LOSE PROTECTION

She spends more and more time writing letters. Specific letters in support of specific individuals. One attempt to contain her sense of helplessness and guilt.

Each request from the sanctuary center comes with a template, but she takes care to make every one unique. She foregoes the computer to write each letter by hand in her wobbly script, an indication of effort and sincerity, she thinks.

Dear Honorable Immigration Judge:

My name is Elizabeth Miller. I am a US citizen. I am writing to respectfully urge you to release Marcos N (Case No. A# 0....), from detention...

I have the good fortune to have always lived in the city in which I was born. Marcos *was forced to flee his country 30 years ago. Six months ago, he was torn away from his wife and 2-year-old child who rely on his financial support.*

Marcos works two jobs, yet he makes time to tutor children in English, his second language. As a parent and as a former ESL teacher, I well know importance of his remaining with his family and community. The separation of families is not what our country, built on immigrants, is about.

Donations, petitions, letter writing take up most of Betty's mornings. Three afternoons a week she doggedly works out at a nearby gym and shops for groceries and the like. Occasional evenings, weather permitting, she attends lectures or panel discussions at nearby libraries and bookstores.

It wasn't long ago she had dinner with Sally, one of her friends who still goes out evenings. They'd descended a few steps to an outside table (quieter). The feet of pedestrians were at eye level. The shoes! Stiletto heels, thigh-high boots, three-inch platforms. Been years since they could wear such shoes. The occasional dog on a leash poked a quivering wet snout through the café's railings.

Give up dinners with Sally and a few others too,? Give up the gym where she's greeted by her first name and told she's amazing for her age? (She wishes they'd leave off the age clause.) Give up her park view, bookstore and library events?

She closes her eyes to listen to the familiar sounds that sift to the tenth floor through double paned windows: a hand cart grumbles along the sidewalk, car door slams, airplane murmurs by, siren wails in the far distance. People talk, shout, sing in different cadences and languages. Give up city sounds?

Move to an institution with dementing and dying people?

Dementing. To dement. A noun become a verb. Platform is another. Only the first three cars will platform at the last stop. Which part of her will platform as she dements? And where?

Is there an actual brook at Brookhaven? Deep enough to drown in? Stop. Make the best of whatever will be.

She reminds herself that she's a highly privileged individual who has been spared the first-hand terrors of war, spared massive injustices and senseless losses.

ROHINGYA REFUGEES LIVING IN LARGEST REFUGEE CAMP IN THE WORLD

Not that it helps. Her situation is hers, and hers alone.

That first act of flight just before migration is painful, almost unbearable. Nothing can rid the bird of such pain but the rapid flight of its wings. (W. H. Hudson)

Living day in and day out with a stranger meddling with her possessions, meddling with her life, and reporting her fumbles and slipups to her children—is equally dismaying.

Hovering. A live-in aide hovering. Like Nancy used to accuse me of hovering. Not Michael. Sweet Michael, too sensitive of others for his own good. I worry about him. But not Nancy. She can look out for herself! Don't hover, Mom. Stop hovering, Mom. Got so I could hardly be in the same room with her. Now she's the one who hovers. Thinks she's in charge, can tell me what I can and cannot do. No longer needs to be rebellious. I humor her. Trade off. Now Nancy thinks she has to take care of me, she can love me without restraint. Be worried about me, be concerned. Concern. Yes, concern suits her.

Suits me too, come to think of it. I've always been concerned about somebody. First the children, then the homeless, and now immigrants. I'm more like Nancy than I imagined. Why the need (compulsion?) to worry about others? Power trip? Think about that another time.

The live-in stranger would likely be a woman forced by dire circumstances to leave her own home and family. Bozena, the cleaning lady (on whom Betty now relies to climb a ladder to replace light bulbs in high ceiling fixtures among other chores) shows her pictures on her cell phone of the children and grandchildren she's left behind in Poland. One is of her son, his wife and little daughter standing in front of a house under construction. A house, a home, where they plan to live out a life, a life Bozena is distanced from. Yes, they Skype almost every day. Skype! Pixeled sound and sight, not cuddles and hugs and kisses. Bozena can't feel the hot breath of a child's secret whispered in her ear, can't feel a soft sticky hand holding her own, can't feel the chubbiness of a body in jammies as it snuggles against her for a bedtime story.

Yes, there would be women in Bozena's circumstances working at old folks homes (institutions disguised as resorts), but they wouldn't be in her home, doing her labor, a daily reminder of the thousands of families torn apart every day, wailing children wrenched from mothers as they are deported ... sisters, brothers, lovers, husbands, wives all cleaved asunder.

RETURN TO HARD LINE ON IMMIGRANTS
TRIPLING OF ICE FORCE

It was only yesterday she read of a baby pulled off a nursing mother's breast. The baby a citizen, the Honduran mother not. Were there dribbles of milk rimming the edges of the infant's gummy mouth? Trickles of the unsuckled trailing down the mother's breast?

Was the baby her firstborn? Michael was Betty's first-born, the first she held close to her heart sleepless night after sleepless night pacing back and forth across a room. Shush... shush... shush... until tears dissolved into little hiccups and soft drowsy breathing. Michael, the first she bathed in a plastic tub on the kitchen counter, hands slithering carefully over his smooth, soapy skin. Michael, the first to give rise to a love she'd never known existed, a love that ached almost to bursting, a love so intense it still brings tears to her eyes remembering it.

She loved Nancy too, but Michael was the revelation that such emotion was contained within her.

Bozena comes only once a week for four hours. Someone every day and night showing her pictures of faraway loved ones? No. Someone telling her what she can and cannot do, telling her she cannot luxuriate in a bath with scented oils (a pleasure strictly forbidden by Nancy). No.

Betty had vowed to live out her life in the three-bedroom divorce-settlement apartment with its high ceilings, decorative moldings, and hardwood floors. You'll have to get me out feet first, she'd said. How long ago was that? Michael was six and Nancy was three when Stanly went AWOL with Elaine. Elaine who happened to be—to have been—Betty's best friend. True to character, Stanley took what was closest at hand, most convenient. His secretary was an elderly woman.

No mortgage on the apartment and that of the upstate house she bought on her own has been paid off. It's just a small getaway that the children cram into on weekends and holidays. She's a guest there now. She resented their takeover at first, then she was glad to be relieved of the responsibility of keeping up the property, glad not to feel obliged to shuttle back and forth because it's there and paid for (typical privileged guilt). She was always forgetting something in one place or the other.

≈

A phone call from Nancy: a one bedroom in Brookhaven has become available. You could move in a month, she says. It's already empty, just needs fixing—painting, new carpets, some repairs. It has a balcony and a lovely view of the lake. There aren't many like this. I've put down a deposit. You have ten days to decide. Mom, I want you nearby and the children will be so happy to see you more often. Soon they'll be off to college.

Off to college.

Alberto took great pride in attending the recent graduation of his oldest daughter from Brooklyn College.

TRIPLING OF ICE FORCE

Dear ICE Officer:

I am writing to respectfully request Alberto not be deported. He came to the United States 40 years ago at the age of 10. He barely recalls the country he left and no longer knows anyone there. His US-citizen parents and US-born siblings are all in the US. His children and a grandchild were all born in the US. He took great pride in attending the recent graduation of his oldest daughter ...

Ten days! A one bedroom! What will happen to her belongings? Furniture, paintings, books, and the contents of seven closets, every last one stuffed with god knows what.

... not be deported ... not separated from children ...

For each person expelled from the US, a remaining friend or family member is told to pack the deportee's bag and bring it to ICE to be thoroughly examined. It can't weigh more than twenty-five pounds. This is what people leave with, the only belongings they start over with. A few items of clothing, maybe a photo or two, a precious letter, a Bible. Belongings, longings, of the unbelonged.

What would Nancy pack for her? And Michael? They wouldn't make the same choices. Nancy would be practical: spare set of clothing, sunscreen, sunhat, extra pair of reading glasses and yes, family photos. She would pack pictures of the kids, include a few of the obligatory shots of them grouped together at Christmas. Michael also would include photos. Maybe even one of his family dog knowing how much she dotes on him. And he would slip in a couple of Betty's most cherished objects. He would tuck in the tiny bronze statue of Tara, Buddhist goddess of peace and protection, the mother deity he had given her for her seventieth birthday. It always sits on her desk.

Would know to pack Leonard's little wooden parrot that also sits on her desk, head cocked sideways, round eye staring out at her? Balefully? Quizzically? Or merely attentively?

She'd resisted moving in with Leonard forty years ago. He'd suggested buying his own apartment in her building and she squelched that idea too though the children were all for it. Leonard, a tireless social worker, her only meaningful love affair. If a couple of others also lasted several years, it was mostly due to inertia.

Leonard called her Elizabeth. With a Z, he said, like "zany," not S. Never was she Betty to him. She didn't call him Lenny as did most others. Formal names were a sign of affection between them. Nicknames and abbreviated names are supposedly indications of familiarity, but not always.

She'd wanted Leonard back. Too late. He'd already married Eleanor on the rebound. She likes to believe he called her Ellie or Nellie or some such diminutive. Meanspirited, she knows.

Leonard died quietly in his sleep, she was told. He always was a gentle, unobtrusive man. Was ninety by then, had lived a long life. Betty hadn't seen him in years, and yet she misses him, misses knowing he's somewhere not too far from her. His a good death, not a tragedy, she reminds herself.

IMMIGRANT CHILD DETENTION CENTERS BECOMING DEATH CAMPS

NO. No way. If she decides to leave, better a stranger, not her children, help figure out what to bring and what to leave behind. Michael and Nancy are both minimalists: sparse monochrome furnishings with only a few carefully positioned paintings and objects in keeping with the general composure of their décor. *Décor, decorum, good taste, propriety. Decorous.* Her children are the decorous offspring of a mother whose home has always seemed to them dismayingly cluttered, scattershot, flustered. Like her mind. Increasingly like her mind.

Visual company. Not only the little Tara and Leonard's parrot, every single object has its associations and memories. Artworks and vases and bowls and heaps of brightly patterned cushions and rugs of all colors, shapes, and sizes are visual company. It's what the children see as extraneous stuff that keeps me company in my increasingly solitary life.

So then. Sorting is up to her. Take control of what's left to control. Second in line for a one bedroom! Ten days to decide! Plenty of time before having to move. She's not fleeing a home destroyed by a bomb. No erupting volcano, no giant tsunami wave, no mudslide, no avalanche is forcing her immediate eviction. She's not a Syrian refugee who has to pack a knapsack in a rush when forced to leave everything behind, even family members. She doesn't have only an instant to decide what's essential, what matters most. A prayer book, a hat, a photograph, medicines?

She's not being packed into a train for *that* final solution. Betty's not Jewish though everyone thinks she is. Most of her friends are Jewish. Leonard was Jewish. Upper West Side of course.

... *polar bears scrambling on the ice chips.* (Gabrielle Calvocoressi)

She's not a polar bear standing on an ice chip. Polar bear or not, she needs help.

Nothing can rid the bird of such pain but the rapid flight of its wings.

Letting out a whoosh of breath, Betty looks up professional moving and organizing companies on the internet.

The photographs, oh god, the photographs: neatly pressed, color-coordinated clothes hang obediently in immaculate closets, rows of shoes prop tenaciously on minimalist racks, jars and cans stand at attention in kitchen cabinets. An invasion of zombies or a plague of toxic orderliness has wiped out all humanity.

She books a "discovery call" from CLUTTER BEGONE. At least the name is ridiculous. And, unlike one site, it does not offer to help "get control of the problem that's controlling you."

Problem? How insulting. She's not a hoarder. Doesn't save old newspapers. Doesn't save tiny bits of string like the multi-millionaire stepfather who didn't leave her a cent. You never know, he'd say, jamming a couple of inches of twine into a drawer. Rich. That's a thing about old money, people can't bring themselves to get rid of stuff as if what they got by merely being born could be swept away if they weren't super careful. Guilt has a lot to do with it too.

It seems she's barely tapped in a request for a "discovery call" when the doorbell rings. Rings again and then again. Jabs of shrillness. Yes, I'm coming, I'm coming.

She clicks open the double locks, pulls the door open and is faced with a woman, age hovering around sixty, wearing a crisp blue suit and sensible shoes, organization personified.

Hello Ms. Miller. I'm Stacy Robbins from Clutter Begone. I'm very pleased to meet you.

Oh, I didn't think someone would come right away. Not just now, that is.

I don't mean to intrude, however your email message did say you would be home this morning.

I guess so.

I responded saying that I'd come over. I apologize for any misunderstanding.

I must have logged off.

Again, I don't mean to intrude but since I'm here do you mind if we have a look around.

Since you're here, Betty echoes. She steps aside to allow Stacy to enter.

Stacy places her smooth leather briefcase at the exact center of the hall table, clicks it open, removes a blue mechanical pencil and a pristine yellow legal pad.

Is it all right with you if I do a quick tour?

Might as well.

Leading Stacy to the living room, Betty takes in the familiar hodgepodge of it, breathes in its scent of bygone cats and dogs and plants and bodies and rugs and perfumed candles and city grit.

So? There's a hollowness in her stomach as if she'd just thrown up.

Well, we can –

So how does this work? Where do we start? She's interrupting, sounding harsher than intended. I mean, I've never done anything quite like this.

Stacy looks around the room, jots a few notes on her legal pad. Betty glances sideways. Can't make out Stacy's minuscule squiggles.

May I go down the hall to the other rooms? Stacy asks.

Why not. Betty trails after her to the bedroom.

The bed is unmade, patchwork quilt flung aside, sheets rumpled with insomnia, a pillow wadded to support a gimpy shoulder. Betty never makes her bed until afternoon and often not even then. A waste of mornings when she's mentally alert. Mornings are for sorting out her life, for emails, for her journal, for activist letters and petitions. She usually doesn't get dressed either, but the March morning was chilly so she'd thrown on sweats.

10 IMMIGRANTS DIE AFTER HARSH COLD WEATHER

A patchwork quilt tattered to grimy shreds was spread over layers of cardboard on the steps of a church she passed yesterday. Where had the occupant of the makeshift pallet gone? Was he still alive? And before that she'd been careful not to disturb a man in filthy brown rags lying masturbating in a dark corner under a scaffolding.

She draws the covers over her stainless, celibate sheets. Stacy is saying something about linens.

Would they be packed for the move?

Packing. *Stacks of folded longing*—a Terrance Hayes line pulls itself out of context—from his into hers. And regrets, she thinks, boxes of crumpled regrets.

≈

Stacy is moving to the next room: Betty's home office. An old, battered suitcase spreads open on the floor—a corpse awaiting autopsy. A photograph lies on top: she and Stanley holding hands as they race to the town hall to get married. They look happy. They were happy that day. Or were they just smiling for the camera?

Ms. Miller, might you be wanting help sorting out the contents of this suitcase and other such containers?

What?

I was asking if you might need assistance in sorting out the contents of the suitcase and other containers of possessions?

Betty kneels down, slams shut the top, as disconcerted as though the suitcase were stuffed with pornography.

It's family stuff. No, I don't want assistance.

Assisted living with a nurse on every hall? An apartment with its own kitchen in a retirement home would be bad enough, thank you.

Stacy is leaning over her shoulder. She smells of lavender, a soothing scent, probably a job requirement.

Would you care to discuss what you want to do about the kitchen, Stacy is saying.

In the kitchen, a loopy, multicolored, ineffective pot holder made of remnants of clothing hangs from a nail on the wall next to the stove. Afterschool crafts. A Christmas present from little Emily. Or was it a birthday?

Nana, I made it all by myself, Emily asserted even before Betty had a chance to strip away the wrapping to see what "it" was.

You made this all by yourself! I love it and it's just what I need.

I thought you'd like it. Emily's tone was deliberately casual, an affectation after she turned six.

Photo: pot holder just like hers dangling from a shattered wall in a war-ravaged city. A home destroyed. And the child?

Photo: a little girl in red tights and white t-shirt strewn with red hearts and strawberries hangs tight to her mother's blue-jeaned thigh.

Photo: a toddler in an oversized blue shirt stands crying in a forest of thick legs. He's at eye level with the cargo pants of a latex-gloved patrol officer frisking down his mother's inner thighs.

Stacy is talking. … list of the items you consider selling and what to donate to charity …

You mean now?

If I remember correctly, you said something about having to make a decision in ten days.

Oh no, I can't . . . I can't possibly do that now. I don't have to move in ten days, just decide if I'm going to move. I need time to think about this. You'd better come back another day. Sorry.

I'm here whenever you're ready. Take your time. I can hardly imagine how difficult this is for you. I shouldn't be admitting this, but I'm quite new at this organizing job and you are my first elderly client. I apologize if I've been insensitive.

Oh. I apologize if I've been rude.

No, not at all. And just so you know, I am a very organized person by nature; I've always loved putting things in order and friends often ask me for help sorting things.

I'm sure you're great at your job and I promise to call if I decide to move.

The double door locks click shut. She pours herself a jigger of Jack Daniels, no ice, and takes it to the living room sofa.

This shouldn't be so traumatic. She's already left one home, the home she created for Stanley and the children. She'd painted the walls herself. Each room a different color. A pale yellow, a soft blue, a gentle gray of early morning mist, a pink so faint it seemed white. She'd sewn a slip cover of gray striped mattress ticking for the sofa from the Salvation Army in big-bellied haste to finish before Michael was born. She'd painted the bookshelf facing the sofa the tender green of new growth, the color of the sprouting plants she tended. Other plants of all shades, shapes, and sizes flourished on windowsills, on shelves, suspended from ceilings. She counted sixty at one time.

Now is different. She's leaving a home and a life she'd reconstructed fifty years ago. In the fog of caring for the children and the acrimonious, drawn out divorce, the pain of leaving the home itself was blunted.

Dear ICE Officer ... Alberto came to the United States 30 years ago...

She's down to only a few plants now, survivor plants that are easy to care for. Two philodendron. Hard to kill a philodendron. And two considerate peace lilies that droop their leaves to let her know when they need watering. Yet even without the living greenery that once was, her apartment is still alive, vivid, and welcoming.

Maureen, it was petite, fizzy-haired Maureen who came into her living room, spread her arms wide, and exclaimed, Ah, the home of a life well lived. A life. Her home is filled with the belongings of a life, pieces of a topography only she can piece together.

Books! Ceiling high shelves of books. Many with penciled notes in the margins. Novels and poetry mostly. Bring the poetry books, even if it means storing some with Nancy. Classic Greek plays too, some with my notes from high school. Moby Dick to reread. And Shakespeare, of course. And . . . so many she can't do without even if she hasn't read them for years and may never open them again. Maybe she should stay put and live with the immigrant hired by Nancy to spy on her.

Should we have stayed at home, wherever that may be? (Elizabeth Bishop). She chose to leave. Walked away from three homes. Three loved homes, she wrote. But not into an old folks home. Never for Elizabeth Bishop. Homes in France, Brazil, Maine. In the end she died in her own apartment in Boston: cerebral aneurysm.

For so many it's not should we have stayed, but *could* we have stayed, Betty reminds herself.

VIOLENCE DRIVES IMMIGRANTS FROM CENTRAL AMERICA

A selfish, spoiled woman. That's who I am.

Yet the feeling of loss is there, a weight in her chest, a clog in her throat.

Guests, a revolving door of guests, felt at ease in her apartment, whether for a drink, a dinner, or a weekend. She didn't fuss, left it to them to uncork a bottle of wine, make a bed, a cup of coffee, come and go as they pleased. So many are no longer alive or if they are, they are in no shape to go anywhere. Some are stuck in old folks homes.

Diane died. A long time ago. She was fifty-five. A linguist who became a photographer to befriend the gypsies whose folk tales she chronicled. Folk takes that Betty helped edit and gather into two books to be published postmortem. Books that would also have to come with her.

Azra died young; cancer like Diane. Azra, Diane. Betty could probably go down the alphabet with friends who are no longer of this world.

B for Mrs. Block, the sprightly, articulate German woman across the hall. After a few years a live-in aide moved in. One time the aide rang Betty's doorbell for help getting Mrs. Block up from the floor onto her walker. Mrs. Block and the aide are long gone.

C for Charlie from the seventh floor, a minister, a man of the collar, a collar he no longer wore by the time his shrunken body was in blue jeans that almost fell off him. Always a short man, he was reduced to the size of a child at the end. A lonely old child.

Neighbors whose names she never knew like the plump, old actress who wore a hat covered with shiny, round buttons promoting past political candidates and other merchandise. She'd sit in the lobby for hours chatting with the doormen and whoever would stop by. She had a fuzzy little dog. First the dog died, then she did. Heartbreak? A tall black woman who was a singer died. Betty didn't know her except in passing. Saw the notice in the elevator.

Betty's is a vanishing population in a vanishing planet. Dying out like the spotted owls and butterflies and bees.

Healthy young friends are gone too. Mia moved to a big house in New Jersey with her new baby and three dogs, Shari to Baltimore for a new job. Renters have been priced out; also owners as monthly maintenance fees escalated. Doormen have gone after years of service. José returned to Peru with his ailing wife. Went back of his own volition.

RETURN TO HARD LINE ON IMMIGRANTS

Endings. TV shows ended their runs, some after years. *I Love Lucy*—gone. Long time gone. *The Wire* and *Homicide: Life on the Streets* are recent departures.

Familiar storefronts are shuttered. The one that sold African wares—gone. Last week Henry's, her beloved neighborhood restaurant where the tables weren't squished together, closed forever. Lincoln Plaza Cinemas. Gone. Favorite clothing stores and the thrift shop on Amsterdam. Gone. Everything is online. Food online. Movies online. Clothes online where you can't feel a fabric between your fingers, can't know what a shade of blue might actually be.

You can't even call anyone anymore. Betty texts her children. Call your pharmacy, her elderly doctor said. Talk to your pharmacist. Good luck speaking to other than a robot these days even after navigating a labyrinth of prompts. She tries to keep up: Instagram, Twitter, and Facebook accounts. Sites she never uses. She doesn't belong in this new world. Better to be among the forgetful ones of her own generation. Lost generation. The phrase takes on new meaning.

She's getting weaker; can't lift the big watering can when it's full. Can hardly open and close the old windows. She wouldn't have the strength to pull Mrs. Block up from the floor these days. Her hearing is weaker too, especially on the right. Even with hearing aids, conversations in restaurants are almost impossible.

Aides. Stay where she is with a live-in aide when she hardly knows anyone in the building? All her new neighbors are busy young couples with small children and more on the way. They text on their phones in the elevator and lobby, discouraging even a friendly hello.

And her apartment—three bedrooms, separate dining room, eat in kitchen—way too big now that the children hardly ever come for an overnight. Things are always breaking down and the maintenance is always going up.

CHILDREN COMMIT 85-YEAR-OLD MOTHER TO ASSISTED LIVING

Not worth reporting, but a headline in the story of her life. And yet, a one bedroom all to herself in a residence where everything is taken care of and help is a buzzer call away might be a relief. She'd have lots of company among the lost generation.

Dear Honorable Judge, I am writing to respectfully request that Graciela be granted asylum status and allowed to stay in the United States. I do not believe that she should be separated from her three U.S. born children, husband, and the community that cherishes her.

... separated from her three children ...

Betty's children and grandchildren would be close by. And they're worrying themselves sick about her.

Why not move? She's had a good run.

As she's having dinner, she hears the wail of a saxophone coming from the park: Izuro! A flight along ascending and descending notes, a flurry of wings. Two months ago his face was slashed from mouth to earlobe and his sax stolen. Thanks to fellow musicians (and Betty too), he has a new instrument. It still hurts, he told her, and then played another riff. A quavering, a tremble, a small cry of release. A homeless man in pain who has nothing and gives everything to his music, gives everything from his music. He's going back to Japan. His brother has booked him a ticket home. Izuro and his jazz evensongs will also be gone.

Betty puts down her fork, gets up to throw on a jacket and go to the park to let Izuro know that she too is moving, that her daughter has booked her a smaller home elsewhere.

≈

Michael suggested a transitional weekend in the upstate house after her apartment was emptied and selected belongings moved to Brookhaven. Just the two of us, he said. She doesn't tell him that halfway through the dismemberment of her home, she'd stopped caring what came or went and left most decisions up to Stacy.

He drives her in what had been her car (she was glad to be rid of that responsibility too). As he turns into the driveway, she notices that lilies of the valley have spread further along the north side. Their brief sweet-scented florets bloom under the earnest shade of scrappy young oak trees.

Rhizome roots, she tells Michael, those little lilies over there have rhizome roots, roots that don't go deep into the ground. They just spread outward barely beneath the surface.

Interesting, he says.

Even if the roots are cut apart into pieces, she continues, talking beyond the patient boredom in Michael's voice, they give rise to new growth.

... Graciela .... three U.S. born children, husband, and a community who cherishes her....

Is this about you, Mom?

No.

No?

Maybe, but not only.

... Sergio become a respected member of the community ... in the restaurant business for 12 years ...

The terrain must be hospitable, Betty adds.

THE WORKINGS OF JOY

Henry Landsdorf was tickling Eloise. Stubby fingers stroked her plump belly to squirms of delight. His touch, delicate as a stray wisp of hair, belied the bulk of his six-foot-three frame bending over her tiny, furry body. Her silver nails flitted the air, nails as long and shiny as Leticia's, the cashier at Dunkin' Doughnuts where Henry got his coffee at 5:30 a.m. every weekday.

≈

He knew Leticia's name because he had asked. Henry made a point of addressing people by their names. "Good morning Leticia!" he'd say.

"Mornin' professor. How you doin'?"

Leticia always called him professor. She'd seen him in a white lab coat. Henry never corrected her. Their brief exchanges did not warrant explanation.

"Good. How are you today, Leticia?"

"Hangin' in, hangin' in there."

In the beginning, Henry mentioned the weather, but the topic never elicited a response. Sun and rain, heat and cold were unspoken between them. But he always thanked Leticia for the coffee. A sign of respect for her profession.

≈

Of the four hundred rats Eloise was Henry's favorite. Not that he ignored the others. He was exemplary in the execution of his Tech B Level duties, diligently checking each creature for signs of illness or injury and maintaining careful records of every animal's diet, weight, medication, and behavior. He dispensed just the right amount of food and a daily supply of fresh water. Their cages were impeccably clean and the Rat Facility rooms shiny white.

Tickling was not a requirement of Henry's job. He'd been at the same Tech B level for twelve years before he began tickling. It was not even part of the research. Henry was The Lone Tickler.

It started on a sunny April Fools' Day. He was sitting on a slatted bench in a little park across from the lab munching the ham and cheese on rye his wife Jean had prepared. A sandwich as dry as she is, he'd thought, and made a mental note to add mayonnaise next time—to the sandwich. Although? But no, never with Jean.

Pigeons pecked in the dust at his feet, their feathers iridescent pinks, greens, and grays in the sunshine. And an oversized oddball with pale brown and white feathers. You're beautiful in your own way, Henry whispered, leaning down. A discarded newspaper lay on the ground, slightly yellowed by sun flickering through tender leaves. It was open to a photo of a man smiling through his well-trimmed beard. He was holding a rat. FOR SCIENTISTS LAUGHTER NO APRIL FOOLS' JOKE claimed the headline.

Henry put his half-munched sandwich back into the small, insulated lunch bag (turquoise, a gift from Jean), velcroed it shut, and picked up the paper.

> *Biomedical research ... rats tickled to study the effects of laughter ... high frequency ultrasonic vocalizations electronically amplified ... 50-kilohertz ... rush of dopamine to the brain ... positive affective state ...*

Positive affective state … I study the workings of joy, the man in the photo was quoted as saying. The workings of joy! Henry uttered aloud, for once mindless of who might overhear. The study of joy, he said, savoring the words.

Back at the lab, he googled "tickling rats" and surfed through about fifty of 925,000 entries. (He'd eventually visit all the sites and keep up with new postings.) He logged on to YouTube videos to watch official ticklers tickling and listen to the rats' chirping, inaudible to the human ear, but amplified to the fifth degree in laboratories and on the internet. Like the rustling of tissue paper when opening a fragile gift, Henry thought. Sounds, he learned, different from the sharper 22-kilohertz vocalizations rats send out in fear or pain. He tried to hear his rats' laughter when he tickled them, bending down close to their sleek heads. He couldn't pick up the faintest sound, but from the motion of their tiny mouths and the twitching of their whiskers and tails, he knew the air was full of supersonic chuckles.

"Don't worry, I know you're laughing," he told Eloise and the chosen ones. He wished he had a rat's sublime, high-speed laugh. He wished he could chirp to his heart's delight without being overheard by predators. Cats, dogs, foxes, lynxes, weasels, eagles, owls, and all species of hawks are deaf to the joy of rats. Not so Henry's predators. They would hear his sounds of gaiety if he did not stifle them. They already thought he was a bit off. He knew that.

Eloise was one of the six Henry singled out for personal attention, giving them names; names he kept to himself. For everyone else in the lab, the rats were the coded sum of vital statistics on labels clipped to their cages. Eloise was R.S/G.F.S.UT-143.

Henry didn't notice the acrid odor of rodent urine and feces that no amount of scrubbing would eradicate, but he always showered and changed into uncontaminated clothes before heading home. Yet, even after dabs of Old Spice aftershave, Jean would wrinkle her nose at his I'm-home-honey peck. "Varmints," she'd mutter.

She'd visited the lab once. "Pew!" she'd said, the word more of a spit than an enunciation, her lovely face contorted into a model of disgust straight out of Darwin's *Expression of the Emotions in Man and Animals*, a facsimile of which was on Henry's bookshelf.

Henry read up on olfactory modalities. He learned that women are more sensitive to odor than men, their anterior insula particularly activated. But his research couldn't erase his sense that Jean's reaction had more to do with him than with her anterior insula.

He never told Jean about the tickling. Nor about the half dozen rats he chose to favor, although in a moment of weakness he was tempted to tell her about Mike, B.M.B.UT-58. A big oaf of a rat, Mike was usually ostracized. Not because of his size, Henry figured, but because he was blind. One of the control group blinded to test the importance of ipRGCs (intrinsically photosensitive retinal ganglion cells) to migraine. That's what the research was about—migraines.

Henry was grateful it wasn't cancer. Yes, the rats suffered, but they had reprieves. What ailed them wasn't fatal, although the experiments often were.

≈

Henry formed his group of six around the time the twins, Lucy and Stanley, turned eleven and DO NOT DISTURB signs appeared on the doors of their rooms, doors that were slammed with increasing frequency. The house shuddered to amplified music from behind the DO NOT DISTURBs. Once outside their personal fortresses, the twins grafted iPods into their ears.

He and Jean met with teachers and checked parenting books out from the library. He consulted a therapist, she a priest. You've over-stoked their self-esteem, concluded the therapist. Do the children still go to mass? asked the priest. Both therapist and priest assured them it was just a phase—the twins would survive over-stoking and irreligiosity. Henry and Jean considered getting a dog, but with no idea how that might help, or, with Jean back at work, who would walk it. Certainly not the twins.

"How about making drawings of your feelings," Henry proposed to Lucy, following a suggestion from one of the parenting books.

"Dad, cut the touchy-feely crap! You're acting like something's WRONG with me. Just so happens I need privacy and I like to HEAR music."

At least he hadn't approached Stanley (Stan The Man) with touchy-feely ideas. He'd even agreed it was OK for him to get his ear pierced and offered to take him to have it done. Jean had a fit.

"How could you not consult me? she yelled. He's MY son too, you know, and I don't want him going around with holes in him. Next you'll be telling him to get a boyfriend!"

"I'm sorry," Henry said, "I should have asked. But he'll do it anyway so I figured better to be supportive on things that don't much matter."

"DON'T MUCH MATTER! You encourage my son to go around looking like some dropout and you say it doesn't matter!"

Dropout! Henry felt his pulse quicken, heat rising to his face, neuronic activity going haywire. He turned his back to Jean, muttering under his breath, Not the worst thing that could happen to Stanley.

"What are you mumbling about?"

"Never mind."

$$\approx$$

When Henry rustled into the laboratory in his sterilized baby-blue paper gown, cap, and booties, the chosen sextet would scurry to the edges of their cages, all pairs of round black eyes—except Mike's, of course—fixated on him. Who would be first to be tickled by his chubby hands? Henry was attentive to the rotation of tickles and he gave each rat equal time.

When he was feeling in need of gaiety, he headed for Judge Judy, R.ST.F.S.UT-148. She was the most vociferous, her jaws quivering with supersonic, ratty laughter. Henry could not keep from chortling under his breath as he burrowed his fingertips beneath her salt and pepper fur stippled with blond streaks—an effect he knew many women spend a small fortune to obtain. Long hairs sprouting from Henry's bushy eyebrows flicked. Despite Jean's urging, he refused to have them trimmed. She gave up eventually, but he never excluded the possibility that she might snip them off in his sleep. She used to like his beard. "Makes you look distinguished," she'd said. Later she complained it was too scratchy.

For affection, Henry turned to Eloise. She was the only rat to give Henry nibbles and licks and she was the most elegant of the sextet—soft, silvery fur, long white whiskers sprouting from a delicate pink nose, exceptionally petite rosy ears. Eloise had a crush on B.M.S.UT-73, Marcos, an energetic brown rat with round protruding ears like Alfred E. Newman's. Henry grudgingly admitted to Marcos' appeal.

R.CL.F.S.UT-111, Gertrude Stein, a calico rat, the most insistent and repetitious, tried his patience at times, although she was the rat with the most character. Gertrude would hit on Eloise, who would have none of her, so Henry put them in separate cages. Afterwards he felt sorry for Gertrude. Holding her in one big hand, he gave her a long backrub with the other. She enjoyed it more than he expected.

B/W.M.S.UT-69, Casanova, sleek and black, gleaming white chest and belly, also hit on Eloise and all the others, re-gardless of sex. Henry put him in a separate cage, but every so often popped in Judge Judy. (He'd tried pairing Judy with Mike, but she'd have none of him.) Judy produced two litters of eight each. The average size would have disappointed Casanova, if he knew. From time to time, Mike got it on with Casanova.

Henry abstained from stroking and tickling when any-one was around, but the rats got so slap happy it was hard to hide. He was caught several times.

"What are you doing?"

"Tickling." Henry was incapable of lying. "It's done in major biomedical research."

"Here we're studying migraines, not giggles."

"I just want to make their lives a little happier." Henry was careful not to qualify the rats' lives as brief and tortured. No sympathy for sympathy in a lab.

"Next you'll be giving them orgasms," quipped Joe.

Joe was an assistant researcher who had almost completed his degree in neuroscience, one Henry had begun to work towards when he started at the lab, but had quit after the twins were born.

≈

Lucy and Stanley were probably conceived on his and Jean's honeymoon, the first time they had sex. It wasn't anything like he'd imagined. That was to be expected, he reasoned later, her being a virgin, eighteen years old, Irish Catholic and all. Not that he was an expert. At twenty-two his experience was limited to a few drunken tussles with fast girls at college parties, all squirmy and slithery. Jean lay perfectly still, but as he was almost done she cried out, "It hurts!"

"I'm sorry, I'm so sorry," Henry moaned in the middle of an orgasm he was unable to stop. There was blood on the sheets, something he'd read about, but didn't think actually happened. Before the wedding, he'd planned to sing "Some Enchanted Evening" after consummation, but, in situ, he scrapped the idea.

That a child, never mind two, would result from this copulation seemed unlikely to him, if not impossible. Even more unimaginable were the complications that followed. Twenty hours of labor and Jean's uterus perforated during the final moments of delivery. She was in the hospital for a month with infection after infection. In the third week, she asked the doctor to tie her tubes and called in a priest for confession. She told Henry only after it was done. He was sitting beside her bed, holding her hand.

"I won't be having any more babies."

"Sweetheart, why? What happened?"

"I had them do the operation, the one that stops you from having babies."

"Why? You'll get better, you'll get over this."

"I don't want more babies. Ever."

Henry looked down at her hand, limp and pale against his ruddy palm. He shifted his gaze to the orangey bottles of pills on the bedside tray, the white tissues crumpled beside them. He focused on a plastic glass almost emptied of water, sucked out through a clear straw bent at the top. He rose and walked numbly to the men's room. Isolated and enclosed, he sat on a toilet seat and wept. He was an only child. Jean came from a family of ten. He'd planned to sit at the head of a table of at least four children, better still, six.

Composing himself, he returned to Jean. "Isn't it lucky we had two at once," he said, smoothing her hair back from her forehead and planting a kiss on the spot he'd cleared.

"Thank you," Jean murmured. "I should have told you, but I was afraid you'd talk me out of it. I can't end up like my mother. I just can't."

For almost a year, Jean was unable to lift and carry Lucy and Stanley, never mind go to work. Jean's mother couldn't help; her youngest was only four. Henry took on a second job, weekend nights as an aide at a rehabilitation center, earning slightly more than the nanny. An advanced medical degree was no longer an option.

The year was a blur of exhaustion—scurrying rats, insomniac patients, crying babies, weakened wife . . . "The best year of my life," Henry told Jean. "You're nuts," she replied. "It was hell."

He'd loved caring for his babies, the sounds of their suckling grunts at the bottle, the slither of their soapy skin when he bathed them in the green plastic tub on the kitchen counter. Most of all he loved carrying a crying infant close to his heart, walking back and forth across the carpeted living room singing "Some Enchanted Evening" until tears dissolved into little hic-cups and soft drowsy breathing. When he straightened up after laying the little sleeper in its crib, it was as if a part of his own body had detached and he was the lesser for it.

Caring for Jean was also deeply gratifying. There was a sense of purpose and worth as he adjusted pillows for maxi-mum comfort, brought her mystery novels from the library, and concocted her favorite three-layered lemon Jello. "Did you hear me singing?" he'd ask. "I was singing for you too, you know."

"I know," she'd said softly. "You're a good man, so good to me."

His father, Karl—first generation immigrant—was fu-rious. "Stupid! How could you be so stupid! No son of mine!" he shouted. "Worked my fingers to the bone so you could have a better life! *Alles für dich! Alles für dich!*" Henry didn't know German but "everything for you" was a phrase he learned along with "mama," "papa," and "juice," the last being his third spoken word according to his mother. Karl was adamant in withholding help, not that Henry would ask. "You made your bed. You lie in it," he admonished. "Worked my fingers to the bone . . . You made your bed . . ." Karl prided himself on his knowledge of American idioms.

He forbade Henry's Polish mother, Jagoda, to lend a hand (lending a hand being another of Karl's Americanisms). Not that she could have helped. Lifelong malfunctioning synapses clogged her spirits with inundations of muffling grayness that made the most basic tasks gargantuan. Forced walks (Karl's idea) did little to lighten the weight of her chronic despondency.

In retrospect, Henry saw his aborted degree and his Tech Level B Nobody status as sublime revenge for a childhood of spelling drills, history quizzes, math quizzes. Revenge for the basketball hoop over the garage too high for a little boy, for the leather baseball mitt too large for a little hand unable to hang onto the hardball hurled by papa.

At thirty-four he still could have become Somebody. The twins were in school and Jean had completed the college degree she'd wanted more than anything else and earned a paralegal certificate too. Overnight she had tailored suits, crisp blouses, high heels, and a regular paycheck. It was she who was Somebody, brisk with achievement and confidence.

"You don't have to work nights at the rehab anymore. Go back and get your degree," she urged. "I did."

You didn't have to add that, Henry thought, but kept it to himself.

"I'm happy doing what I do," he told her. "Why put myself through the stress and exhaustion of grad school? I'd still have to keep my day job."

What he didn't tell her was how important his nights at the rehab center had become. Hovering at patients' bedsides in rooms illuminated by flickering monitors and the dimmest of lights, his head bent close to catch whispers of the sleepless, he was transported, weightless, to another state of being. Not that he was religious. He went to church with Jean from time to time, but the experience was more one of endurance than spirituality. The center was his cathedral, its resurrected bodies his salvation.

He became attached to certain patients during their long nights of wakefulness. Indomitable Mark, eighteen, with a spine like the beer cans he used to crush with one hand. Old Mrs. Thomas riddled with rheumatism and lame jokes that always made her husband laugh as if hearing them for the first time. Paralytic Consuela whose grown children and raucous grandchildren came to visit every evening.

Henry thought of quitting many times—for Jean's sake. She liked to go out on Saturday nights. Date night, she said. He'd tried taking her to a movie in the afternoon and an early dinner, dropping her at the house before heading off to minister to his patients.

"It was not the same," she sniffed. "The restaurant was deserted. The sun was still out."

"I'll take you out on a weeknight. How's that?"

"The kids have homework. School the next day. Same for babysitters."

Gradually the problem went away. Jean found friends for Saturday night outings.

"Who?" Henry asked, curious. It didn't occur to him to be jealous.

"Other mothers from school and the playground."

"Their husbands work nights too?"

"Single mothers mostly. Divorced."

As for grad school, everyone would be younger than me, Henry thought. This too he kept to himself. Lee Yoon, an intern in her mid-twenties—pale wisp of a girl, like a shadow on a gray day, who simply did what she was told—had already written her first article for *Nature Neuroscience*. At thirty, Edith Kaprow, rapier thin and ambitious, degree in hand, had published ten articles, mostly co-authored—but so are the majority of scientific writings—and she had a book forthcoming with MIT Press.

"My work is as essential as anyone else's," Henry insisted to Jean. "The research wouldn't be possible without the animals in perfect condition."

"Taking care of rats! What sort of career is that?"

"I live a life, not a career," Henry shot back.

"Suit yourself."

"That's what I'm doing."

He didn't add that his job was fun, playful; that genetically engineered rats were sensitive, clever, and affectionate, nothing like the dark rats that forage among garbage. And that even those have an undeserved bad reputation. He never told her how rats love to laugh. Certainly not how good he was at making them laugh. He's sure they wouldn't have laughed for Edith, and not as heartily for Lee Yoon.

Instead he would tell Jean about research at the lab. He used the first person plural in such increasingly rare instances. "We've just determined the ipRGCs are important to light sensitivity in migraines."

Jean's expression was uncomprehending.

"Photosensitive retinal cells. We've discovered that clear and grey lights make headaches worse," Henry elaborated.

"I could have told you that," said Jean.

"Now that we've traced these nerve pathways in the brain, hopefully we can develop new treatments."

"Hopefully? That's it? Hopefully."

"It's all research. That's what research is—a search. We don't know what we'll find. Otherwise it wouldn't be research." Henry was aware of his voice rising to unusually high decibels, amygdala out of control.

"Suffering. It's about freeing people from suffering," he said softly.

≈

It was after Henry abandoned his degree that he gradually came to realize that Jean had thought she was marrying a Somebody. They'd met at a reception for incoming graduate students in the science department. Henry caught sight of her standing alone in a corner of the wood-paneled reception room crowded with academics holding on to wine glasses and theories. He stood gawking. Pale skin, no make-up, wide blue eyes, jet-black hair. A quick inventory took in plain black pumps, a severe black skirt falling primly to just below the knees, and the contradiction of a creamy satin blouse slithering over full breasts. A black velvet band studded with rhinestones circled a smooth coil of hair at the nape of her neck.

Taking a deep breath he made his approach. "I don't believe we've met."

"No."

Henry persisted beyond the monosyllable, keeping his eyes fixed well above the gentle rise and fall of her satin blouse as he introduced himself.

"Jean O'Connor," she replied.

"Are you new to the university?"

"I'm not with the university."

"I'm new here, so I don't know who's who yet," Henry apologized. "I've only met a couple of people at the lab."

"You work in the lab?"

"Part time. Part of my scholarship deal. I'm a first year student. Neurobiology. It's a field that's getting more and more attention, even on TV."

There was an awkward silence. Henry didn't know what to make of it, only later thinking that Jean might have been afraid of saying something stupid.

"Um, can I get you some wine? Some cheese?"

"No thanks."

"Seems like we're having an Indian summer."

"Yes."

"Well, enjoy the evening. Good talking to you."

The next time Henry saw Jean was in the supermarket. She was behind the cash register, encased in a green canvas apron, Central Market embroidered in white above her left breast. He placed peanut butter and jelly, English muffins, frozen corn and peas, frozen French fries, and a steak on the conveyer belt. He regretted not having chosen fresh vegetables, organic humus, and Greek yogurt.

" Jean? Right? I remember you from the reception."

"Yes."

"Bachelor life . . . busy schedule," he mumbled as she rang up the total. "Going on a diet next week," he added. A harried woman behind him, cart piled high with provisions topped by a screaming baby, squelched the possibility of further conversation.

"See you soon," Henry said, grabbing the bulging brown bag. (At least he'd thought to ask for paper, not plastic.) And he did see her soon and often, figuring out her schedule and timing his trips to the market accordingly. After a few weeks of conveyor belt courtship, Jean accepted his invitation to dinner. She broke up with the registrar who had invited her to the party where she and Henry met. The registrar had gone off somewhere and left her stranded for an hour. He had a habit of being late, Henry was to learn.

"It's nice that you're always on time," Jean told Henry on their third date.

"Punctuality is very important in my family."

"Mine too, Jean said. There are so many of us we don't have time to wait on anyone. Show up or ship out."

"That's funny. My father always says, Shape up or ship out."

New to town, Henry was living in a small attic apartment hastily rented from an elderly widow. Half-unpacked suitcases and boxes of books spilled their contents out on the floor. He had to crawl under the eaves to reach most of his things. Only at one end of his one room could he unfold to his full height. If he forgot where he was, which happened often, he'd bump his head getting out of bed or up from a chair. The Widow had a no-women-allowed rule and Jean had a not-ever-in-any-man's-apartment rule. The closest she came to his tiny garret was the wide wraparound porch of the house and the front door with its elegant, stained-glass panes.

≈

Henry placed Jean's macaroni and cheese casserole in the microwave. She was working late again. He put two plates on the kitchen table in front of the iPodded twins. They briefly looked up. He was grateful for that flicker of acknowledgement. Once again, he was surprised to see himself and Jean incarnate in the two, but with sexes reversed. It was Lucy who had his reddish curly hair, stocky build, and pale blue eyes. Stanley was all Jean, even to his dark hair pulled back in a ponytail.

He put his own plate on the table and opened a well-thumbed issue of *Neuroscience and Biobehavioral Review*, flipping to "The Neurobiology of Positive Emotions."

Signals indicating that bodies are returning to equilibrium . . . ancient sub-neocortical brain regions we share with other animals . . .

Remembering Lucy as a tiny little girl, Henry asked if she still liked to be tickled. He knew it was a mistake as the words came out of his mouth.

She detached one buzzing bud from her ear. "What?"

"Never mind."

"What? What is it?" Lucy insisted.

"Just wondering if you still like to be tickled."

"Dad!" she groaned.

"The question is scientific. Research has shown that laughter in rats produces an insulin-like growth factor chemical that acts as an antidepressant and anxiety-reducer," he explained.

"Gross," she muttered, leaving the room and her half-eaten portion of macaroni and cheese.

≈

That was the year Jean would go ahead to the lab's Christmas party while Henry finished checking on the rats. When they were first married, she'd been reluctant to accompany him, but as time went on she seemed to look forward to the event. That year she was exceptionally excited by the prospect, her words tumbling over one another. "I'll be fine. Know people who'll be there. Take your time. See you later. Bye. Bye."

As he entered the room, his eyes scanned the crowd in search of her. She was standing in a corner, the same corner where he'd first caught sight of her thirteen years before. She was wearing a red silk dress. A clinging party dress he hadn't seen before. Her hair was loose, falling in waves to her shoulders. She's put on weight, Henry observed, and wondered why he hadn't noticed the beauty of her new fullness until this moment.

Close by her was Edith Kaprow. They were laughing. Except for a little grating sound that was more of a snicker, Henry had never heard Edith laugh. He was surprised by the deep, throaty sound issuing from her thin, sharp body. Jean's counterpoint laughter was bouncy, gleeful, also unfamiliar to Henry. Vibrations traveled across the room. No need for amplification.

They drove home in silence, walked in silence from the cold garage into the warm kitchen. Still in his dark winter coat, standing in front of the glistening white counter, Henry turned to her, his arms limp by his side. "So?"

"I've fallen in love," she replied, heading back towards the garage.

He blocked her way. "Jean, Jean. What . . . Please. What are you doing?"

"Do you realize this is the first time you've looked me full in the face since I don't know when?"

"Maybe I've been a little distracted, but I never meant to ignore you."

"A little distracted! You've been avoiding me. For years, you've been avoiding me. Things were great when I was helpless, just a little Nobody, but it's been downhill ever since. You didn't even come to my graduation last year!"

"There was an emergency at the lab."

"Ah, an emergency! A rat! Henry to the rescue."

"I'm sorry, so sorry . . . I took you out for dinner afterwards."

"Yes, but you didn't see me get my diploma. You weren't there."

"Why haven't you said something?"

"I've been too tired, tired and busy with the kids and school and then work, just taking one day at a time. Then someone began paying attention to me. Me. Jean. Do you know that Edith came to my graduation?"

"Edith? Edith Kaprow? Why?"

"Because she found out you weren't going to be there. She knew how important it was."

"So that's when it started."

"More or less. We'd gone out to dinner a couple of times, nights when you were working. But yes, that's when it started. When someone special was proud of me, saw me, saw who I've become."

"I've always been proud of you, Jean. You're the one who never thought I was good enough."

"I did, but you gave up. You went off to your damn rats and gave up."

"It's not like that."

Jean turned away, heading up the stairs. "It's late. I'm going to bed."

"I'm coming too."

"No."

"You want me to sleep on the sofa?"

"That, or I can leave."

"Stay. Please stay."

He didn't bother to open up the Castro convertible. Taking off his shoes, he lay down fully clothed, using his coat as a blanket. As always, he fell asleep immediately. When he awoke, rumpled and sweaty, the sun was brutalizing his face. An announcer on the radio was breathlessly reporting a plane crash that wiped out an entire soccer team. Jean was click-clacking in the kitchen, every step a slap. The digital clock on the cable box below the TV read 7:00.

He heaved himself up and called out to Jean, "What are you doing?"

"Getting the kids off to school."

He shambled into the kitchen. "Can you stick around so we can sort this out?"

"I've got to get to the office."

"Call in sick. I will."

"No. We'll meet somewhere after work. Then come home and tell the kids."

"Seems like you've already sorted everything out."

"There's not much to say. Just logistics."

"That's what all these years together have come to? Just logistics."

"I'm only trying to get through this. Believe me, never in the world could I have imagined . . . the last thing I expected . . . You've been good to me, Henry. I'm sorry. I'm so sorry. I feel terrible. You don't deserve this." Pathways of tears began to erode her carefully applied makeup.

"No," he said. "No, I don't deserve this." For once, he couldn't find it in him to comfort her. He wanted to shake her, shake hard until she cried out and came to her senses.

At the lab Henry went straight to Eloise before checking food and water supplies. As always, she hopped up and down in anticipation of his touch, lifting herself upright to grasp a high bar of her cage, soft belly descending pear shaped to tiny pink feet, her long pink tail extended for balance. The skin of her little rosy hands (Henry never called them paws) glistened under the fluorescent lab lights. "Ready for your tickle?" he whispered in her pink ear. She licked his fingertips.

≈

The twins are sixteen and have their drivers' licenses. Jean and Edith have bought them a car. Henry no longer has to pick them up on alternate weekends.

Stanley sports a rhinestone earring, Lucy a tattoo of a mermaid on her back. Henry has complimented them on both. Stanley tells him about his rock band, but doesn't invite him to hear it. Lucy tells him she's writing stories. "Maybe I'll let you read one someday," she offers.

"I'd like that, Henry says. I'd like that very much . . . when you're ready."

The therapist and the priest were right. The phase is phasing out. And he has time to wait for the next developmental stage. Four years of coming home to an empty house have tempered his understanding of Darwinian evolution.

Five of his little band of favorites ran the course of their brief rat lives not long after his marriage had run its course. Eloise lived the longest, but then she too died. Taken off to another part of the lab she was anesthetized, her trusting eyes injected with Green Fluorescent Protein. Usually the rats would awake in mute endurance of brain splitting migraines. He added extra bedding to her cage, but by the end of the day she had not been returned.

"Where's Eloise?"

"Who?"

"The little gray rat you took away this morning."

"Eloise? You said Eloise?"

"I sometimes give them names."

"You give all of them names?"

"No, just a few . . . sometimes. A way to pass the time."

"Whatever. She didn't make it. Sometimes they don't. You know that. Dissection table 5 if you want to take a look."

"No."

≈

The lab has been shut down for two years, the migraine project ended. Without a significant breakthrough funds dried up. Four hundred rats were euthanized, all nameless. Henry hadn't the heart to name a single one after Eloise died. He'd occasionally give a rat a soft tickle, but mostly out of habit.

He now works six nights a week at the rehab center and spends his days trudging between classrooms and libraries studying for his Physician's Assistant degree. He'll soon be almost a doctor. Almost. His choice. And it suits him just fine.

FLY SPY

Fly flies in from the cold. Spy fly? Cat spies fly. Mission: capture fly. Belly flat. Tip of tail twitch. Leap. Fly spy flies out to the cold.

THE END

About the Author

Julia Ballerini was born and raised in Latin America and lived many years in Europe. As an art history professor and critic, she published books, essays, reviews, and curated exhibitions. She also directed the educational program of a drug rehabilitation center for homeless women. Since 2010 she has turned to writing  fiction. In keeping with her life, her teaching, and her writing on documentary photography, many of her stories are about understandings and misunderstandings across languages and social customs and within families. Some protagonists are elders confronting failing health and mortality with trepidation, courage, humor, and adaptation.

For more information, please visit my website:

www.juliaballerini.com

Acknowledgements

I've benefitted from workshops led by Cameron McDonald, Christopher Sorrentino, Stephen Wright, Lori Segal, Ann Packer, Helen Lee, Fiona Maazel, and Ella Peary. As an art historian coming to fiction writing later in life, I had much to learn from instructors and fellow participants alike. I owe a special debt to Cameron McDonald's insistence on getting every word and punctuation mark to do its job. For their patient and astute readings of many stories over years of multiple drafts I thank Michael Bennett and Caitlin Campbell. Susan Ransom has often generously volunteered her meticulous copy editing skills. My thanks to Maria DiBattista and to Sally Sevcik who were kind enough to read through early drafts of *The Unforgotten* when it was a novel and to Sandra Newman who, years later, suggested ruthless cuts to pare it down to the novella it became. Ella Peary has been a precise, thoughtful editor of the collection as a whole, and has become a friend in the process.

I've learned a great deal about writing from several reading groups, most recently those ongoing remotely at A Public Space led by Yiyun Li, Elizabeth McCracken, Garth Greenwell, and Carl Phillips. Twitter and Zoom comments by leaders and readers have been humbling revelations.

I am also grateful beyond words to those family members and friends who have upheld me through rough, it's no good, give-it-all-up times. You know who you are.

This book would not exist were it not for the validating YES! replies from journals that published the following stories.

"Gloria," *Persimmon Tree* (2012)

"Top Secret," *The Tishman Review* (2015)

"Departures," *Flash: The international Short-Short Story Magazine* (2015)

"In a Castle in France," *2 Elizabeths* (2017)

"Luisa the Unforgotten," *Bare Fiction Magazine* (2018)

"Descent," *Linea* (2018)

"Environmental Lapses," *The New Guard VIII* (2019)

"Painless," *Rue Scribe* (2019)

"Ultimatum," *Wordrunner* (2019)

"Penance," *Remington Review* (2019)

"What Do You Feel," *Streetlight* (2019)

Made in the USA
Las Vegas, NV
14 May 2021